FOXES IN THE SPRING

SECOND IN THE VERENDEN WORLD OF BOOKS

NIK FULTS

FOXES IN THE SPRING BY NIK FULTS

The Second Novel In The Verenden World Of Books.
The Precursor To The "Froh'v" Trilogy Of Books.

"WITHIN VERENDEN" PODCAST

LISTEN TO NIK FULTS DEBUT NOVEL, SISTERS OF BLOOD & FIRE, FOR FREE ON ALL MAJOR PODCAST NETWORKS.

LEARN MORE AT AUTHORNIKFULTS.COM

THE VERENDEN WORLD OF BOOKS

Sisters Of Blood & Fire

Foxes In The Spring

Copyright © 2020 Nik Fults
All rights reserved.
Paperback ISBN: 978-1-9990580-1-2
Ebook ISBN: 978-1-9990580-2-9

ACKNOWLEDGMENTS

Cover Photo by
  Filip Bazarewski
  Artstation.com/bazar
  Flip.bazarewski@gmail.com

Songs & Poems of Verenden,
  Written by Varshaa Ragu, C.M.Baxter, & Nik Fults.

To A:
"It's just us."

And To A Few Creative Individuals That Shape Me Into A Better Person & Writer:

Brian W Foster & The Entire Critical Role Cast
Brandon Sanderson
Neil Druckmann
& Troy Baker

GODS & GODDESSES

Lwo: Gatekeeper of Death.

Keeper: Giver of Life

Brenuin: God of Wealth & Luck

Dormer: Goddess of Love

Areya: Goddess of War

Anseris: God of Death

Verenden

The Islands

Slimhixe

The Icy Sea

Deaths Port   Olgierdum

Summerland

Klibia

Veritas

The Islands Of Verenden

Frost Meridiem

Ignis

Fornicace

Aestas Isle

Mare Point

Dulacas

Verenden

The Islands

Slimhixe

Triumpth

Remorse

Boneshiver

The Icy Sea

Deaths Port

Olgierdum

Shadowfalls

Olgierds Rum

Softsand

Wickeds Trading

Lowlands Luck

Rilea

Lummerdum

Veritas

1

A CHANGE IN PACE

No father should ever smell the smoke in the air and fear it is that of his child. No father should ever have nightmares recounting the times he ran through a city square just in time to see the last of his son's tears sizzle away with his skin.

No father should ever have to remember the screams. The crowd cheering as everything you ever deemed perfect in this world is taken away from you in a mere minute.

No one gets to choose whether or not they get a quirk, but when you have spent nearly all of your life helping an empire that will one day murder your child in front of you and your wife . . .

It takes a toll.

A toll on my marriage, a toll on my heart, a toll on my hand whenever I pick up a blade and feel the weight of my son upon it. Never knowing if in my lifetime I will ever be able to avenge him.

I wish I had told him I loved him one last time. I wish I had held him. I wish Amarille and I could sing to him one more time as he slept.

For it was, at the age of ten, that my son unwillingly first sprouted a flame from his fingertips.

I still remember his eyes, the realization on his face upon seeing me just in time to watch him burn but too late to save him. I still remember the charcoal smell and the feeling of being powerless to save the only thing that truly matters.

For it was, at the age of ten, when he was turned into ash upon a wooden spire where hundreds every day meet that same fate.

Slimhixe, an empire I used to call my own…took my son from me.

I remember it all.

I will never forget.

And I will avenge him.

For Erron.

* * *

"Back so soon?" my father calls out to me. "I do hope my friends were not a disturbance."

"Actually, they kept to themselves a lot," I say, bringing him into a quick hug.

"Yes…that does indeed sound like them."

"You are a long way from The Frost Meridiem?"

"Amarille invited me over…haven't been here since the wedding so I assumed not much had changed." He looks around the dock and back towards the house at the top of the sly mountain. "You know, you would make a fine architect if you weren't—"

"Better with a sword than I am with a hammer?" I smile. "Shall I lead you inside, old man?"

"Is that any way to speak to **your** old man? One whose name you share, Vesten the 2nd," he chirps with condescension.

"Is there any other way?"

"I can think of a few."

We laugh, and I take his arm, guiding him away from the dock and looking back towards my ship.

Snow hit the tops of the large sails. The unnatural lack of a crew was apparent. Of course, I had already dropped them off south of here to the top of Klikia where most others who sail reside. With their pay, they can afford a few nights until I sail off to the next destination. Knowing them, they are probably making the kegs dry by now, sharing stories, and lying with as many men and women as possible. *Talons Tread* is a fine ship, built nearly all by hand, much like my house.

"Winter's come early," I say. Feeling the brisk air hit my face, no doubt causing it to become red like my hair.

"Well, I imagine after spending some time on a trade route to Summerwind, all of the time in the warmth takes away the frostbite."

We walk back up the stones. I see the smoke at the top of the large hill. It feels odd seeing this home again after a while, almost foreign. I remember placing every stone down by hand, trying to think of ways to incorporate having horses near the base, making sure Amarille had everything she needed.

"How is Amarille?" I ask. "I hope not too mad I was gone?"

"She'll be madder if you are gone while she delivers your **next** child."

I stop walking, removing part of my grasp from my father and watching his eyes widen at the realization. "I am sorry," he says with a cough. "I did not mean to bring up any loose feelings."

I nod and continue leading him up, now approaching the front door after the steep, uphill climb. I open it to hear the sound of crackling fire in the centre, the extreme warmth hitting my face. The wind from outside now more calming as opposed to irritating.

Amarille walks in, Clutching her pregnant stomach with both hands and smiling wide when she sees me. She approaches at her fastest pace to bring me in for a hug. Her long red hair is up, revealing Elven ears that point to the ceiling.

"Mind if I borrow your library, dear?" Vesten says.

"Our home is yours, Vesten. Borrow all you'd like." She smiles, lifting an arm up to escort him, but he refuses.

"I am away from those dastardly steps. I will be more than okay."

With that, he takes his leave and slams the door behind him. The room on the left is a library and workplace for Amarille's documenting and writing. The room on our right leads to the outside courtyard with fireballs floating above our crops. And, of course, the room in front is our bedroom.

"Hello, beautiful," I say.

"You look like shit," she says back in a sweet voice.

"Well, the seas will do that to you."

"Don't remember the seas asking permission to ruin my husband's face."

"Nor do I." I lean in and kiss her.

Walking with Amarille to our room, I take a look outside and see the archery target placed near the end of the crop field, arrows lodged into it.

"You shouldn't be using a bow while this far along," I say with a laugh.

"Well, if you were here more often, maybe I would begin to listen to that advice. This child has taken away a lot of what I love. I won't let it take that away."

"You could still use a cr—"

"Besides, a crossbow is nothing more than pointing and shooting… barbaric honestly."

We walk into our bedroom. The large bathtub in the centre of the room with the fireball pit to its side still just as ugly as I remember. Of course, Amarille thought it would be a lovely idea to put it right in the centre and as her husband, I dare never to cross her. Nevertheless, I hate it.

"Do you have any news about…" I ask softly, treading lightly as to not bring up any unwanted anger.

"The change of political leadership? No," she says.

I help her sit down on the bed and then sit across from her. "I am sorry, I know it can't be easy to find a job in Summerwind as an advisor."

"We just need one big act…something that can more than prove our newfound allegiance to Summerwind."

She takes a second to herself, gently rubbing her stomach before staring at me with her green eyes. "I just…wish this life was behind us both. That you had no more need to set your sails."

"Aye." I reach out and grab her hand. "One more job…then I will be back and be able to continue supporting our family."

"I keep having nightmares," she abruptly says. "Dreams in which you are there but not…I run and nothing. I try to interact and—"

"Nothing." I move to sit beside her and lean her head onto my shoulder. "Did these dreams start after—"

"Erron," she brashly says. "Yeah."

We never talked much about him. I mean *why* would we? It was never something that I felt had to be addressed. Our son, gone. Forever feeling as if a part of our marriage was taken by the fires of Slimhixe with him. It wasn't long after that we switched empires, cut off all loose ends, all connections, all friends. Why should we be expected to support an empire that burns children for being born with a quirk?

Everything reminds me of him: this house, my sword, Amarille's eyes, which he shared. He was no more than a boy, no more done learning than he was living. And yet…he was taken from us.

I still remember building this house, placing down each step, not for myself…but for him. Building a crib to place in our room while I planned to build a nursery. Now we have another child on the way, and we know where our allegiance lies.

"I have been having those dreams as well," I whisper. "Where everything feels normal…until it doesn't."

"I am not going anywhere." Amarille kisses the side of my neck.

"Neither am I, Amara."

* * *

WE ALL GATHER around the table I dragged into the main library for us to sit down at for dinner to eat some type of bird I never asked about. Like usual, it's a clean-killed animal that Amara found on the end of an arrow. Luckily for us, once I return, I will bring us countless piles of food so she will no longer have to hunt.

Time is moving so fast. She's already getting further into the pregnancy than first expected. We thought by now we would have switched empires without feeling the end of the dagger on both.

"Any news on a gender?" My father breaks the silence.

"The Mender says it could be either, nothing for sure yet." Amara smiles.

"How are things at Eaforith, father?" I watch him smile after being called father.

"Busy, like usual. Gwen and Kaya, who you had sailed to Eaforith, will contact me soon for employment."

I widen my eyes. "You are to leave The Frost Meridiem?"

"They are to start an orphanage...for quirks. A safe space." The table goes silent with his words.

"You sound mad," I say while Amara gives me a look. "That type of thing would never last."

"Darling—"

"The only safe space for people with quirks is the ground." I clench the kitchen knife in my hand.

"Darling—" Amara tries once more to call out.

"It does not matter who they follow, people with quirks don't get to live fucking easily—"

"Vesten!" Amara places her hand on mine, using her other to guide my face to look at her.

I stare into her eyes, now noticing my hand still clenches the blade, and my adrenaline pumps loudly with my heartbeat, like I'm in a sword fight.

"Look." Father stares at me. "I know I wasn't here a lot for Erron, but I assure you I will be much more active from now on. The moment your new child is born, I will set sail and come here to help."

"That really isn't—" Amara tries to chime in.

"It is," he scoffs. "I am a busy man. I still recall, not long ago, Vest barely wanted me to attend his wedding. It is true my husband and I were not around enough for you, but I assure you I will never disgrace this family again."

"Vesten, Headmaster of Eaforith...now a family man?" I say seriously but laugh like it's a joke.

"Vest, you are right," he says. "There will never be a safe place for people with quirks. Not without pain, struggle, and tribulation. But together, as a family, for your new child, we can do our best."

"What was that saying? Your family motto?" Amara looks like she has an idea but won't say.

My father, confused, starts, "A fox in the spring—"

"Travels without a choice," I finish. Turning to Amara, I say, "A reference to the lack of foxes during springtime due to the influx of—"

"Duggandrowls, Lycans," Amarille interrupts and shoots me a look of disapproval. "Clawfiends, Bruckbears. Darling? Have you forgotten I hunt during every season?"

We all laugh. "It's a good saying and if it means anything more..." She looks over at me and smiles. "I never get tired of seeing foxes before they hide away."

Vesten smiles. "Our family used to mean so much, loyalty, love, strength...I fear we have forgotten our ways."

Amara puts down her utensils. "Fear not. I will assure our new child lives by those words." She leans back in her chair and rubs her stomach. "My family came from money, but it clouded their sense of family. City elves without a motto or real sense of background...it would mean more than enough to carry on both of yours."

I watch my father try to subtly wipe away a tear from his face, laughing at his own showing of emotion. "Thank you, Amara."

Before long, dinner is over and it is soon time for bed, no sound but the crackling of fire in the entire home. Amarille is keeping to her books, and I stay sitting in a rocking chair built for her. My father comes into the library and sits in front of me, just staring into the embers as well.

"So one last job?" He breaks the silence. "And my son will be back to being a family man?"

"I am always a family man."

"Aye, you are...but this isn't an easy job like you are trying to fool her into believing, right?"

"What do you mean—"

"Your fabled crew couldn't stop talking about it while they picked me up. Big stories of sailing east to pass through Klikia and eventually go into the city portion of Summerwind?"

I refuse to lie. "Aye, that is the plan."

"You know as well as I do that is essentially a fool's errand."

"You know as well as I do, Vesten." I snarl slightly. "That I have less of a choice...if I do not at least prove my crew essential enough!"

"You cannot afford that type of risk."

"I can afford whatever it takes to get back to Amara!"

"The waves will tower you if you take that route!" He snarls back.

"You risk everything? To what? End up as dead bodies on Death's Port with the others who dare believe their ship is mightier than the gods?"

I don't respond, instead opting to bite down on my tongue.

"You know I am right, son. Take the easy route, it is surely better than risking yourself and crew? Do you want Amarille to become a widow?"

"Bite your tongue, Vesten!" I stand up in my seat. "How dare you bring that sort of talk into this home? Tomorrow, I sail for Klikia, southeast, and deliver the package. Back in a few days to continue being a better father than you and Dad."

He simply gasps, peering down at the fireplace before nodding his head and leaving me by myself with nothing but the crackling fires while I clench my fist in anger.

Who is he to tell me that I can't sail east? Many have done it before and lived to tell the tale, and I will surely become the next. Traveling east will be much faster than west, and the crew and myself will be able to easily navigate the rough waters.

I do feel bad about lying to Amarille, guilt that I suppose won't go away until I return home. Back to our family so that we can once more be complete, I won't have to leave much after that. Only a day to go for food or a morning to ensure we have enough firewood.

I take one last look at the fire before turning my body and walking into my bedroom. The glass windows shine the night orb's light into the room while Amarille simply reads on the bed next to a candle. She must be able to tell I'm angry as the second she sees me she looks worried, her smile fading, her eyebrow tilted.

"Darling?" she whispers.

"Yes?" I reply coldly.

I suppose she can also tell I'm in no mood to talk. She knows me better than anyone, after all. "Come here."

"Why?" I say.

"Don't ask why. I am your wife, and I demand you come here!"

I dare not disobey, walking over to the bed and lying down on the pillow beside her as she sits up. "Stressed?"

"Very," I say as she moves my head onto her legs and scratches the top of my head. "I said some things to my father I shouldn't have."

"Well, you are known for speaking your mind." She giggles to herself. "You two are at a tricky situation. You didn't have him growing up as much as you'd like, and he regrets that. You two will get in fights, but it is only because you love each other."

"I promise I will not be long away," I whisper.

"I know, you never are."

I raise myself up slightly, and she kisses my lips. Often I hear people complain about kissing the same person over and over after marriage. For me, it feels like the only time I'm ever truly happy.

"Just remember, everything I do, I do for us," I say.

"And just remember," she says, pressing her forehead against mine, "if you die, I will fucking kill you."

We laugh in the dimly lit room. I lift myself up and onto the backboard of the bed, reaching my arm around Amara's shoulder and pulling her in close.

I'm going to miss this feeling of warmth and home. The smell of her hair, and the feeling of her touch.

"Do you remember when we were younger?" I say. "Out in the back of a peach farm in Summerwind? I would climb the fence just to come see you."

"I remember you running as soon as my father would send the hounds." She snickers. "But I also remember meeting you every night at that one tree at the very end of my property. I remember intentionally missing shots with my bow so you could get close and 'show me the proper way.'"

"Oh yeah...how come you don't 'miss' around me anymore?"

"Cause you were a boy, and I like you knowing how much better I am than you."

2

PEOPLE WHO SAIL EAST

Waking up in the morning to the sound of my beautiful wife throwing up is not something I particularly enjoy. Running over and helping her, I make sure to get anything she needs while it seems she becomes a vessel for a demon that requires specific food and nutrients to survive.

Once I make sure she's okay and properly tended to, despite her basically doing everything on her own, I walk into the living room. My father is sitting on the rocking chair reading a book on quirks and fables. He makes eye contact with me and smiles. I can tell, however, that he doesn't fully mean it. He's still mad after my comments last night. Why wouldn't he be? I do not get a pass on saying such things because I am of his blood.

"Good morning," he says. "I made some tea and put extra in a pot." He motions towards the fireplace where, on a small metal grate, the large kettle sits near the side to heat but not boil.

"Father," I say. "I am sorry. I know you did not deserve my words…sadly I fear my tongue is sharper than my mind when it comes to saying things."

He grins. "Nothing you said was not deserving. I accept the fact I was not always here for you. It is a mistake I must live with, not you."

"How long will you be staying?" I ask, pulling up a chair and pouring myself some of the tea into a tankard.

"Not long, until you return," he says, looking over his shoulder and behind himself. "Did you tell her?"

I shake my head no, and he curls his lips, looking unimpressed.

"Were you ever upset?" I ask, watching him tilt his head. "That I didn't end up with a quirk like your students?"

"Gods no." He coughs. "I was more upset at what it meant. I am—was a headmaster at a place for people with quirks. I knew I would not be able to have a non-magic user around for a variety of reasons. I was upset I could not see you."

"I was in good hands," I reassure him.

"That you were…your father—my husband was one of the best swordsmen I ever met. Used to travel around Klikia fencing for coins. A part of me wished you would have avoided that life." He looks around the home, inspecting the top arches and architecture of the entire place. "But part of me is glad Dennen taught you to defend yourself and our family."

"I used to ask him questions about you…funny, I knew your name but could barely remember what you looked like. Only that we shared the same rustic red hair and blue eyes. He said I got mostly your features from birth."

"Aye I was…funny how magic works. Able to conjure a child for same sex couples that is a perfect match for them. All without having to bear a child for nine months."

"Must be a relief." I chuckle.

"A big one." He laughs. "That's not to say you don't have some of Dennen's attributes. You developed his Klikian accent, his walk, and definitely his sword skills. A perfect copy of two flawed men."

"I am flawed," I reassure him.

"I would dare say you even have **more** than his skills, but gods know he is probably watching us right now."

We laugh together. "He was taken from us too soon."

"Aye…taken in his sleep of all things, peaceful, but I like to imagine if he were awake, he would have drawn a sword on Lwo himself."

"I think he would be proud of us, reconnecting and ending up here. Carrying on our family's mottos and practice."

"I know he would, son." He smiles at me.

I hear the door open behind me and see Amarille enter. I lift myself up to offer my seat, but she grabs her own and throws one into the right place.

"I believe even with a child inside of you, you could still very much kill a bear," Vesten says.

"I believe she could very much kill us both," I say.

"You two would both be very right. I may seem larger, but I can still fire two arrows faster than one of you could snap and the other unsheathe" She laughs.

Amarille is one of the toughest girls I've ever known. I still recall her taking pride in being able to fire a bow better than most soldiers all while wearing a dress. I still get slight flutters in my stomach whenever I see her, like when we were kids and sneaking around. I still think about the first night we ever kissed and how her lips tasted like the peach tree we both sat on top of.

I pour her a cup of tea and hand it to her. "We are talking about parents, any stories?"

"Well, my mother died giving birth to me, and my father owned a large farm. Not to say he wasn't bad, didn't mean to get her pregnant. I grew up on the peach farm, met a boy, and now I am here."

"And your father?" Vesten chimes in.

"No longer with us," she says. "Lived a full life, made good pay, and that was enough for him I suppose."

* * *

THE SHIP IS ONCE AGAIN full, different people, some of whom I don't fully recognize and others who have sailed with me awhile. Berric, my first hand, is in charge of ensuring the entire crew follows his orders to a tee so that I can steer us to making enough money for the lot of us.

Berric sees me and hops off the deck onto the piles of freshly fallen snow. He has one hand over his axe and the other pointing around at my ship. He has large scars across his face and an eyepatch over one eye. "Little girls and smaller boys!" he calls to the ship while everyone looks over. "This is the infamous Fox...Vesten, your captain!" "Greetings, crew!" I wave to them.

"Cross him, and he will slash you across the chest with his sabre!" Berric laughs.

"Aye Captain!" the crew yells in unison.

"Back to work!" I call back, watching them nod their heads until returning to rushing around the ship.

"You look like shit, Captain." Berric snickers, pulling me into an embrace.

I take a look at the new scars across his hand and tilt my head. "Another shark attack? No wait, don't tell me...you were caught stealing another wife's husband?"

"*Berric The Bold Betrothed* to all who live in Verenden!" He laughs. "Actually, this one was from a Flankterror while I was hiding in the deep decks of Death's Port."

"Cuts aren't deep enough to be a Flankterror." I raise an eyebrow.

"Okay fine, a wife found me and her husband in a sauna, came at me with a pitchfork."

"Classy." I put a hand on his shoulder. "You ready for one last voyage until this measly ship becomes yours?"

The ship's large sails are now getting the fresh Summerwind peach tree symbol painted onto them by a few men and women climbing on ropes. The name at the back is faded, the saltwater pressing against the rotted wood that reads 'Talons Tread'.

"This crew seems new?" I ask cautiously, seeing some of the new faces and only a slight handful I can hardly recall.

"Lost a few to the change in leadership." Berric tilts down.

"And yourself?"

"Only in it for the coin and husbands." He laughs, stopping mid-cackle to bow down his head at someone behind me.

"Berric, you look like shit," Amarille joins in the conversation.

"Your husband has informed me, my lady."

Berric bows at Amarille before slightly nodding his head at me and walking back towards the ship.

"He will get you killed one day." Amarille grabs both my hands. "He is known for stealing husbands."

"The tortured souls at Death's Port couldn't take me away from you, Amara." I bring her in for a hug, taking one last moment to smell her hair and feel her stomach.

She pulls away from the hug and presses both her hands against my stubble. "Be home soon my *Froh'v*."

One of the only elvish words I know: Fox. I tried learning the technical way of speaking her High-Vidicium, but it became far too complex for me to follow along with. Instead, she opted to teach me simple words.

I press both my hands against hers, closing my eyes before meeting her face, maybe for the last time.

I begin, "Whatever we do—"

"We do for the advancement of ourselves," she whispers. She looks down at her stomach and releases her hands. "Remember why we are doing this, okay?"

"I will never forget, Amara." I lean over and kiss her gently.

Taking a few steps back and resting one hand on my simple steel sword, I put the other on my heart and then point them to her. I look up the tall steps to see my father standing near the top, simply smiling until pressing one hand to his chest and then lifting it back to me. A simple yet effective way of showing he will miss me.

I head to the end of the dock and vault over the side of the ship, walking to nearly every member of the new crew, and introduce myself. Most of them address me with either 'captain' or 'fox' as a sign of respect. Before I had the rank of captain, I went by the simple name Dennen had used before his passing. I worked my way up from a simple ship hand to captain by talking my way into joining the conversations of higher ups. Eventually, having to duel the captain of a ship, I would rebuild and name 'Talon's Tread'.

I walk up the creaky wooden steps and to the top of the deck where Berric awaits me, holding a map. I place both hands on the wheel and smell the salt water in the air. My nostrils sting with the cold before I call out "Sails!" The ship hands push the ship away from the dock and raise the sails.

We'll have to sail a day before reaching the critical point in which we begin to head east. On that day, we shouldn't have any trouble, simple sailing and easy winds. I simply steer away from my home at the edge of Aestas, looking upon my house and family slowly growing distant until eventually they are no bigger than ants.

"You didn't tell her we are sailing east, did you?" Berric chimes.

"No," I say.

"Smart, she would have impaled us both if she knew." He laughs. I don't say anything, simply keeping my eyes on the blank horizon. The ocean waves, the white from the sky, and the three orbs that slowly move lower and lower in the sky if you pay close enough attention to them. "Have you sailed East?"

"Never," I say. "Have you?"

"Once, actually, when I was naive and young. I was a hand on a ship whose name I cannot recall."

"How did it go?"

"There was this one other ship trying to make their way back to the islands by sailing west from Olgierdum. They jumped on our ship and tried to breach us...as this was happening, their ship was taken in the large waves. The only thing between the one I was on and the bottom of the sea was a lone man at the steering helm...eventually everyone just stopped fighting. We all knew no amount of gold was worth all of our lives. There was some kind of honour in that."

"The man who drove the ship, he still around?"

"Once we docked in Klikia, the crew suddenly remembered we were at a battle. Didn't matter how many beds or food scraps we shared...everyone just began fighting."

"I am sorry to hear it," I say, looking over at him inspecting the map.

"Don't be, learned a valuable lesson that day."

"And that is?"

"Never trust those on and off death's door."

* * *

A few hours have passed and the ocean looks the same as when we first left Aestas, empty. I know that soon I will be able to release the wheel and let the ship simply get taken by the tide. We won't reach any dangers until the evening tomorrow. Most of the crew has gone below deck to drink, sleep, or sing. If I try to mute out the sounds of the wind and ocean, I can hear some of the songs they are singing. *Take the blade from Areya and sail the coursing sea! Forever acquire all those things you seek!*

"It's getting late." Berric walks up the steps to greet me. "You should get some rest, Captain."

"Before I leave, it has been a few years since we last talked. What has been new in your life?" I laugh. Looking over at him, I see his scowl, for once not a sly smirk or chuckle.

"Back at Aestas, I met a man whom I had stolen away from his wife," he begins.

"Your reputation precedes you."

"Aye…this one, however, was different."

"Say it ain't so? Berric actually getting feelings for something other than a coin purse?"

"Fuck you." He chuckles. "I am telling you, this one's something, Vest."

"Well I am glad, surely it must be quite a man to have acquired the interest of yourself." I laugh, beginning to walk away from him.

"This is it, right? One last job?" He presses a hand against my shoulder.

"One last job, my friend…Get some rest eventually. Only the gods know what we are up against tomorrow." I press my hand on his shoulder. "What are we smuggling anyway? Weapons? Ale?"

His eyes widen and he takes a step back as if I'm about to draw my sword. He strokes the scars on his chin and then turns himself towards the sea.

"Best you take a look yourself…Captain."

The tone has completely switched. I raise my arms to show I am not going to hit him like his face says I will. "Berric?"

"Gods give you a good rest tonight…for the both of us, Fox."

I tilt my head and look at him, waiting for him to eventually turn around, but he doesn't. Not even a mumble or whisper. Instead, he opts to just stare. That's not like him. Never in the years we've spent together have either of us been afraid to tell the other person the truth, blunt as it might be.

I hustle away from him and make my way down the top deck and towards the crew, walking away from my cabin and down into the belly of the ship. I hear more laughing and singing below me.

Immediately, I smell alcohol and sweat. Some crew-mates watch two others arm wrestle near the other side and others drink and tell stories.

"Dormer's tits, you are strong!" The man sweats from head to toe.

"Brenuin's cock, you're annoying!" She slams his hand into the table.

I walk over to the table where one man holds a single lit candle and shares a story about what happens after death.

The man notices me and drops the candle, standing up.

"Captain!" he nearly shouts, clearly new to ships.

"Fucking at ease, man." I laugh while the crew joins in. I lean myself against a wooden pillar overlooking the table. "Please, continue your story."

"Aye, Captain." He takes a swig of some ale overflowing from a tankard. "And all souls who are killed go to Lwo's grasp. Only they are still somewhat alive...awaiting vengeance on he who struck them down."

Some of the crew members gasp while a few others simply spit on the floor.

"If that's the case I think we are all fucked!" A woman sneers and everyone erupts into laughter.

I take an empty tankard from the table and pour some of the Ale into the mug.

"Cheers!" I call out to the lower deck as everyone flings their drinks into the air at once and then back down, slamming the table before downing their liquid.

I decide to walk around and simply observe the crew, touching the shoulder of most of the crew as I pass through to show them respect. I walk to the other end of the lower of the ship before seeing a closed door with a handwritten sign that simply says, "Do not enter."

I don't know what we're transporting to Summerwind, but not even royal documents ever carry such a high stature that one cannot even enter. I do not hesitate before opening it with one hand while finishing the tankard in the other, throwing it behind me.

Some people begin to take notice that I have entered the fabled room. The crew as well try to catch a glimpse of what is so important. The room is simple storage, no windows, candles, or other crates. Only one box in the middle of the room with a few holes scattered here and there. I walk over and see how it is bolted dead shut. You would need a few people to open it up.

"Odd," I say aloud.

I hear mumbling and turn around to see the crew getting back to their activities. I look around the room and see no one, then down at the box and tilt my head. Lowering myself down, I press my ear against one of the holes.

I hear crying.

3

DO NOT OPEN

"What the fuck is this, Berric?" I yell on the top deck as he cowers slightly to the corner of the ship. "We are not in *this* business!"

"We are in the business of Summerwind now, thanks to you!" He coughs and lifts himself higher, trying to intimidate me. "And Summerwind wants the fucking box, no questions asked…Captain."

"Fucking gates of death…" I say, heading back towards the steering wheel and kicking the base. "This is not *us*…we are more than this."

"We *were* more than this, Fox. Then we bloody switched empires thanks to you and your wife."

"Mind your tongue! You are not in a position to have the higher ground!"

"I am—"

"If you are not happy with this plan, if the mere idea that the reasoning for us switching sides is not enough for your mind, draw your fucking weapon!"

"Bandits!" I hear the lookout above us scream.

I look over to my side, seeing a small escort ship hoisting the Slimhixe banner in the golden sails. *Fuck.*

"How far out?" I walk down the stairs to the crew members.

"A few minutes," a woman says.

"Can we escape them, Vest?" Berric calls from the steering wheel.

Their sails are bigger and their ship much faster. It grows closer to us with every passing second.

"No!" I yell back.

Berric turns the crew and yells out, "Prepare for battle!"

I watch as the ship steers its way directly towards our side. A few archers take some of the crossbows that lay to the side of ships, firing what they can. Attempting to bear the harsh wind, some get lucky and make contact.

They fling ladders over the side and a few men and women barge onto our ship, wielding a variety of weapons ranging from halberds to axes. The crew all draw their swords and scream, trying their best to fight off the small onslaught of people trying to board. I hear another ladder slam beside my upper deck and see three people rush over and next to my steering wheel and sword.

They hold their swords too low, their axes too loose, and their halberds too high. They're clearly untrained by the intense military. Not that Slimhixe has a good reputation for actually training their soldiers.

"Why are you boarding? We have no wares," I try to reason.

"High value for the prince of Slimhixe," the woman snarls.

"We have no such—?"

I swiftly remember the box. *No, it couldn't be.* Of everything, there is no way we would be trusted with such a high demand. Unless a new ship that wouldn't ask questions would do exactly as Summerwind's government needed.

"We will be needing that boy now," the second of the three snarls.

"You know, I used to don those sails." I unsheathe my sword. A few of them jump slightly. "I used to follow your righteous king and do whatever he asked."

"So, hand over the boy…you know Slimhixe could pay you way more in men, women, and coins!" The third grasping the halberd tries to reason, wiping sweat from his brow.

I place both hands on the hilt of my sword and lift up my elbow, bringing the sword up and twisting it in my palms to face the one in the centre. "Your empire has taken *Everything* from me."

I lift up my arms as if going for the one in the middle, watching him back up before the man with the halberd lunges towards me. I pirouette and twist my body around the curved blade at the top, getting in between the wooden pole and himself and jamming my sword into his gut. He falls to the ground, coughing blood onto the hilt of my sword and my chest.

The one with the axe attacks next, screaming while flailing her axe around herself as if I'm a sporadic training dummy. The man at her side uses nearly the same tactic but with a few more lunges. I deflect both easily enough, removing my second hand from my sword and diving over to grab the man's blade with my hand.

Just before he can pull it any farther through my palm, I jam the sword into his neck and swing myself around into another spin to slash against the woman's chest. Both of them fall lifeless.

"Vesten!" Berric runs onto the deck to meet me. "Need some help!"

Behind him, two men follow holding the typical Slimhixe sword I hold in my own hand. Their leather armour is only a few dyes away from my own.

"Gentlemen," I say to them, feeling nothing but revenge in my blood. I can't help but look at them and imagine Erron at the stake. A dreaded feeling rises in my stomach that maybe my future son will be born with a quirk and be unlucky enough to get ruled under Slimhixe's reign. "Child murderers lay in your empire, along with rapists, and thieves…which ones are you?"

They dash themselves towards Berric and I, Berric using his smaller mace to bash the one man's hand and crack away his bones. The sword clangs on the ground while the other attempts a predictable slash attack at me. Turning my body, I slam the hilt of the sword into the back of his head. He falls to the ground unconscious while the other tries to run for his life, getting to the main deck before a crossbow bolt launches into his chest.

I raise up my sword and jam it into the back of the unconscious one. The only things I see are my son's eyes, the same ones my wife has. I never got the chance to grieve or take revenge. I didn't know if the next time I saw someone donning a Slimhixe insignia that I could simply turn the other shoulder and show mercy...I guess now I know.

The other ship detaches, with it a man on the deck staring directly into my eyes while turning the wheel and attempting to escape.

"Archers!" Berric shouts to my side, the sound of arrows getting loose from crossbows through the whistling wind being the last thing that the captain probably heard before it lodged into his skull.

The ship is now motionless, drifting off, and away towards gods know where. Probably to be washed up on the shore of Ignis, scavenged, and fixed into one better fit for that province's rule over the islands.

"Berric." I walk over to him. "Did you know?"

He smiles at me, looking slightly concerned as I walk towards him faster and faster. "Did I know what?"

I raise my hand and punch his gut, his first instinct being to clutch to his mace before the archers draw their bows back with the sound of tightening rope.

"Did you know we were smuggling the fucking prince?"

He spits onto the ground, sheathing his mace. "Gods, Fox! Of course I didn't know! I knew it was a person of great importance. I knew if we asked any questions they would send a dagger through the hearts of everyone we have ever known!"

"Gods help us all, Berric."

"Gods help **you**, Vesten."

"What did you just—"

"I have fought beside you for a long time, both sides! And I have never asked questions to either. That person I saw fighting on that deck was not The Fox...was not my friend. A captain that doesn't show remorse is one I do not intend to follow."

"You are talking about disobeying your captain?"

"I am talking about you remembering! You are right, we are more than this life...but I fear now that maybe, just maybe, you are trying to bite more than you can swallow. *Erron would not want this!*"

I help Berric back up, biting my tongue so hard I taste the slight tang of blood.

I sheathe my sword and wipe some blood on my trousers before feeling a slight raindrop land on my nose.

The night sky is harsh, very few stars, and the typical orange cosmos is covered by its own sea of clouds in the sky. Bright flashes off in the distance grow closer, along with the first few droplets of rain. Soon a shower pours onto the ship. I know this feeling…the smell in the air…the sounds…a storm.

"We are not done yet, Berric," I yell at him as I rush over to the steering wheel. "Alert the crew! We have a storm to escape!"

I watch him slip slightly on the steps but recover enough to make it to the bell at the base of stairs that he starts flailing back and forth. The loud ringing pierces my ear drums through the sound of thunder.

"Get to positions! You filthy Duggandrowls!" he screams while running all across the bottom deck.

The few remaining people of our crew rush up the steps and slip on the top of the deck, one smaller man nearly sliding right over the edge before Berric latches onto the back of his shirt and flings him back to the centre of the ship.

"Lift the sails!" I demand.

I watch as everyone tries to run their slippery hands through the ropes. The large white sails get hoisted high into the air as the three white long sails resembling sheets are getting pushed by the wind.

The storm is right on top of us now. I watch a few crew members fly overboard and into the ocean screaming for their lives. I attempt to run over and throw down a rope towards them but they are down beneath the mountain-tall waves before I can even see them. They scream their last words while still in the air and the sound of water acts as a final course down to the bottom of the icy sea.

"Hoist yourselves!" Berric screams as loud as humanly possible.

The people on the ship all pull out ropes, wrap them around their legs, and tie that end to the part of the ship they are stationed on. I watch one woman get flung over the top with a large wave and Berric rushing over to grab her. His hand barely reaches her before she is dangling over the edge. He tries his best to lift her up, but before he can, another wave hits us and lifts our ship into the air before plummeting down into the waves. Her grasp is released with the force.

Berric's arm bends in half, broken from the sheer pressure of the side of the ship.

Once again, a scream rises until she hits the water.

Most of the crew is now hoisted in, some of them even latching themselves to one another in order to maintain better traction against the slippery wood.

Lighting crackles and I turn to my side, watching as off in the distance water gets pulled up from the sea and into a swirl, forming multiple small water tornadoes. Another crackle from behind sounds muffled, like it's behind cloth. I turn to look behind us to see a wave, bigger than any I have ever seen before. Larger than any that I reckon anyone would ever be alive to tell the tale of.

It's easily triple the length of the ship. I waste no time before turning the ship away from it as best as I can, making sure my leg is hoisted in tight before the ship gets pushed back first and tilts forward.

"Hold men! Hold all!" I scream.

Slamming the wooden level to my side down with my boot, I watch the sails fall back into the neutral folded positions. The ship gets launched upwards. I feel my feet lift from the ground and watch as everyone moves seemingly with no gravity before they plunge back down onto the deck. In an attempt to break the fall, my head slams against the wooden wheel and my vision goes hazy.

I can't see much in front of me except for a deep fog, trying to focus my vision in all the rain but seemingly failing. My vision shows the rain red, as if it's a thick blood, before finally I regain my sight.

I unhoist myself from the safety knot and jump the top deck, landing on both my knees and leading into a roll to disperse the energy.

"What are you doing, Vesten!" Berric screams to my side.

I feel the water underneath us take a leap like before feeling my feet nearly lift from the floor until I run and slide on my side. I use the slippery water as a lack of traction to get over top of the staircase leading to the lower deck.

My body gets flung up nonetheless and my back is held against the roof for a few seconds before I'm slammed into the bottom deck.

My face hits the small bit of water that is beginning to leak into the ship.

I run back towards the storage room, kicking the door open and drawing my sword.

"Bring yourself to the other end of the box!" I yell just before getting slammed into one side of the wall and dropping my sword. My arm feels numb and loose, clearly not broken, but I'm unable to lift up the sword. My long hair is in front of my eyes so I can barely see.

I use my left hand to pick up my sword and jam the blade into the box's top corner, prying as best I can but failing. It raises slightly but not nearly enough to open the top. Some screws are halfway from being dislodged and the strength of my left arm alone is not enough.

I wipe the sweat from my eyes and press my elbow down against the hilt of the blade and wait. I try my best to keep my feet as still as possible in the small layer of water.

I close my eyes, feeling the waves crackle and slam beneath my feet before I feel my feet once again lift in the air like they have done twice before. My back flies up and hits the roof. I scream and lift my elbow up, waiting until the ship has once again fallen off the wave before slamming my elbow down onto the hilt of my sword, breaking the box's top in two.

The box flings over onto its side and a smaller boy rolls out from it, rope gagged in his mouth, his hands and feet bound. I grab the sword and begin to saw through it to free his arms and then rip the rope from his mouth.

"To the top deck!" I yell at him, watching him anxiously nod his head and run with me up the stairs. The wind pulls my hair immediately to the other end of the deck.

"Vesten! What are you doing?" I hear Berric scream from the side of the ship hoisted to the bell.

Behind Berric comes a wave, larger than the one from before. This one isn't going to send our ship flying upwards and slamming down like the other three...it's going to flip us. It towers over us like the large snowy mountain I built my home atop. A home filled with a family I may never see again.

"Berric!" I scream, running towards him before the wave slams down onto the ship, and I am thrown overboard. I yell something incomprehensible while falling and crashing into the water.

I try and claw my way through the water to make it to the top but my one arm feels incapable of doing anything. I try and kick, but I open my eyes to look up at what seems like hundreds of feet of water between me and the surface.

I swim as fast as I can, the pain in my chest and lungs not enough to stop from me from trying. Eventually, I realize I can't. The surface is too far away, my ship creating a shadow over me as different pieces of debris cover the orbs' light from reaching me this deep in the water.

The water pulls me down into the deep as my arms are unable to lift me any higher up. The sound of crackling thunder and cracking wood from the top of the surface is muted by the sounds of...nothing. Just water flowing, gently, like blood throughout a body.

Slowly, I fall deeper and deeper until I cannot see my own hands through the darkness. I close my eyes and think of Amara.

"Whatever we do, we do for the advancement of ourselves, my Froh'v."

Wouldn't put it past a madman,
Take the wind right out his sails,
For when he follows the rising glow,
his journey's bound to fail

Heed the warning of the lights
Follow them home at dusk
For if your minds wander east,
Consider your fortunes dust

-Luna Varsh, Songs Of Verenden, Tome 7

4

ASHES

The water that coughs up from my lungs burns like molten lava, my hands dig into the scorching hot sand, and the saltwater feels like it is now forever ingrained into my skin. I claw more and more from the water, feeling the tide slowly come back to reach my ankles and the slight fear every time I think I may be pulled back into the deep. The water, of course, isn't nearly as strong as before.

The storm vanished in the time I spent in utter black, and still I crawled faster and faster away from the sea as if a chain should emerge and grapple me back down to the depths. Once I am far enough on the scorching sand, I turn myself onto my back and look up towards the crisp blue sky. A few birds fly above me and squawk to one another. The three orbs absolutely destroy my skin with their blistering heat, and for a few moments I believe I may melt in the heavy layered clothing I wear to keep myself warm in the winter.

I try to breathe from my mouth and feel the dryness on my lips, my breathing sounding as if hollowed and sandy like the beach. I begin to throw off my winter clothing, tossing the jacket and trousers away from myself before noticing the few new gashes across my chest and hands. I raise myself up as best I can with the little energy I have but see nothing.

Out in front of me are the open ocean and beach. I turn around to see sandy mountains and grass beyond that. I'm stranded in a place I don't know.

I hear the sound of a slamming wave and see broken, splintered wood wash onto the beach, breaking further on impact with some higher waves. Slowly, more and more things wash onto the beach, less and less distinguishable until a flashing metal sign floats to me.

"Talon's Tread," I murmur as I walk over to the edge of the beach and lift it up.

I look up at the sea of my broken ship, where occasionally a few more larger pieces float and bob from the deep where I imagine the majority of the ship will stay for the remainder of Verenden's days. A few heads fling up from the body of water, with them lifeless and pale corpses that float among the top. No one is alive, not that I can see at least.

"Help!" I hear screaming off behind me towards the sandy mountain covered in grass.

I reach down for my sword and realize it is long gone; my scabbard is laying in the sand with my trousers and jacket. I'm barely covered, let alone ready for any sort of fight.

I walk over to the mountain and climb up. There are small aches and pains in my lower back with each tense footstep. The dreaded heat from the orbs forms sweat all over my body.

Walking to the top of the mountain, I see a small village. A variety of ages all dressed somewhat close to myself to the painful heat, some men bringing barrels of what I assume are fish and ale to the back of horse carriages while some kids practice their sword fighting. I know where I am now…this is Klikia. Where I was born.

This isn't the capital, though. It's much smaller, and I only came here a few times to see someone specific. This is a small trading village called Lowland's Luck.

I look around, trying to find the voice I heard calling for help earlier. I focus my vision on a boy at the bottom of the hill, pleading to people passing by for help. I see his short black hair and recognize him immediately…the kid in the box.

· · ·

I walk down the hill as he continues to preach away at people passing by who barely take a moment to look in his general direction.

"Please! Just a few coins or minutes of your time to get me out of here!" he pleads.

"Boy," I call out behind him, watching him turn around and his eyes widening before he begins to run. "Wait!"

I run after him, making my way through a few people and small straw homes. We find ourselves on a line of fishing huts. I push a few people out of the way before a guard intervenes, his shiny armour donning the symbol of Summerwind's empire: two hands connected underneath a peach tree.

"What seems to be the matter here?" the cold voice demands.

"This is my son." I don't let the child speak. "Our fishing raft was destroyed off the coast in the storm with his mother."

"That is not true!" He snarls. "I am Eli—"

"Autumnspark, and I am his father, Vesten."

The guard eyes us up and down. We're soaked in saltwater. When he turns away and returns to his duty, I grab the back of Eli's soaking wet collar and throw him into the side of two of the homes.

"Are you fucking insane?" I nearly scream at him. "Going around telling people you are the prince of fucking Slimhixe *in a fucking place that is loyal to Summerwind?* Do you want them to hang you where you stand?"

He doesn't answer, only pulls his shoulder away from me to release my grasp and continues on his way through the homes. "Where the fuck do you think you are going?"

"Back home," he snidely comments before trying to walk out of my sight.

"Oh no you don't." I rush after him and grab his shoulder.

"Hands off me, old man, or I'll have you beheaded in the name of the king."

"King's name doesn't work here, Boy," I snarl. "Now do you wanna get out of Klikia or not?"

"This is Klikia?"

"Fucking gods, Boy."

I take a step away from him, rubbing my fingers in between my eyes. *Unbelievable.*

"I need you to take me home," he demands again. "Back to Slimhixe."

I look around at some people passing by. "Absolutely fucking not, Boy. It was me and my crew's job to bring you to Summerwind. You are no longer my problem."

I walk away, leaving him before heading back in front of the homes and making my way to the main square.

"Wait!" He now pulls on my arm, his strength more than I anticipated, causing me to jolt to turn and face him. "You're a mercenary, right?"

"This is a shit fucking plea so far."

"Great! So I can pay you, easily far more than whatever Summerwind would." He smiles, trying his best to show commonality.

"Done." I watch him jump around a little bit. "Give me the money."

He stops smiling. "Well…I don't have it on me right—"

"Then I cannot help you, Boy." I hover over him, watching him cower. "My entire crew is dead and the last thing I need is for my allegiance to be questioned for helping transport a child."

"I am fifteen!"

"I don't care!"

"Please, there's gotta be something you want! There is no way you freed me on your ship just to have me die alone like this!" he pleads one last time.

I pause, tiling my head, thinking about Amara and our child. "I need a clean slate."

"What?"

"A clean slate. I need you to remove the mention of my family's name from Slimhixe's lexicon. So they won't even know me and my wife ever existed, let alone betrayed your side."

"Why did you—"

"Boy." I closed my eyes, feeling the headache in the back of my skull. "Can you do that?"

"Yes, yes, absolutely yes." He reaches a hand out to shake mine. I just grunt and turn away.

"There are ground rules," I say. "If you don't follow them you are on your own."

"Done," he says, determined.

"No talking, do not second guess anything I say. And most importantly, do not tell anyone who you truly are."

"Who do I say I am?"

"Say you are my son, and we are fishermen traveling to deliver products to the city of Triumph."

"We don't have any product."

I tilt my head. "Our ship was just destroyed."

"Oh...right. Well, where are we going now?"

"Are you always gonna not follow through with the first damn rule I gave you?"

I look over at him and see him tilt his head. I guess he has never really been mistreated before, being a prince.

We walk until we find the main town of the fishing market, people with stands and children playing. It's been a while since I've been to Klikia, but after a few attempts, I find the building I'm looking for. A taller one, far at the end of the small town. I had been to Klikia a lot when I was younger and just started doing mercenary work. My friends all used to stay in taverns around here and drink until we forgot which day of the week it was.

I remember my friend telling me about this coin he had found washed up on the beach with a corpse. Not knowing what it was or its worth, he attempted to sell it to a blacksmith and accidentally stumbled onto one of Verenden's best kept secrets, Klikia's true intentions.

Most of the buildings in Klikia looked the same, straw and wood being the main foundations of what made them up. Sand for floors with rugs scattered in hopes to mend it but usually only making things worse. Where me and my crew would usually dock, we would find thousands of tents and ships all bordering along the coast in hopes to trade. Here, there's nothing except my broken ship at the beach.

I walk into the taller building and immediately feel the heat intensify with the burning coals and smell of ash. An older lady hammers away at some burning hot metal until drenching it into some sort of liquid and then throwing it onto a pile of others. She looks over towards us with her giant helmet on to protect her eyes.

"Can I help you two?" she wheezes, letting out a large cough before throwing her helmet off. "Vesten?"

She looks pretty much the same as I remember, pale elvish skin wrinkled now, due to her age, and large blue eyes hidden behind dark brown hair. She never believed in her own age, still making weapons for certain high-ranking people and forever putting herself to work. Because of this, she, in a lot of ways, has more muscle than me despite the age difference.

"Hi Diania, been awhile, hasn't it?"

"How did you know where to find me?" she groans, walking over to a table of weapons and cleaning them with a small sponge. She looks at me and groans once more, now reaching underneath the table and handing me some clothing. A small black gambeson and pants with a small orange stripe going down the centre.

"The best weapon maker in Verenden, at one of the smallest hidden locations of Klikia?" I put on the clothing and nod at her. "My ship is destroyed, and it landed me here."

"In Lowland's Luck?"

"Yes."

"Is that why you have come with a child?"

"Actually, yes. His words are safe with mine," I reassure her, almost feeling the tension of her hand itching to grab a sword and let the unfamiliar face meet his wrath at the gates of death.

"I am guessing you are not here as a friendly courtesy…or because you really needed clothing?" She removes her large gloves and walks over to some already-built swords. "Amarille need a new bow?"

"No, Amarille is fine," I say, scratching the back of my neck. "To cut it short, I need a new sword and a boat to sail for Summerwind."

"That is asking a lot. What for?" She refuses to look up at me.

"The boy…he is royalty."

She laughs. "Perfect! Delivering Summerwind royalty is exactly what I need to further solidify my coin purse!"

"He isn't," I cough. "Summerwind's loyalty…"

Diania's face turns very quickly from a smile into a look of desperation. She raises one hand up as a sign to stay back and picks up a sword with her other hand.

"Vesten, *please,* for the sake of your family, do not tell me you brought me the prince of Slimhixe?"

"My name is Eli!" He tries to demand respect.

"Shut up, Boy!" I snarl down at him before I walk over to Diania slowly with my arms in the air.

"He is with me, he is going to help Amarille," I try to plead. "He won't cause any trouble."

"And how do I know he isn't just going to tell his father about Klikia's weapons? As far as those fucks up north are concerned, we are nothing more than a trading village for fish."

"I won't tell a soul!" he now pleads.

"If I suspected him of that, I would have killed him on the beach when we first met."

The boy looks up at me both offended and terrified. He takes a few steps towards the back door before I reach an arm out towards him. "Do not go anywhere, Boy!"

"Vesten...you know what this means, don't you?" Diania throws her sword onto the pile. "You will become an enemy of both sides of the war. You won't be safe if anyone finds out your true intentions."

"I know," I say. "But if I deliver him, Amarille's name and my name get cleared."

"Fucking hells, Vesten." She rubs her eyes with her greasy fingers, causing some of the black residue to appear underneath the bags of her eyes. "All of that work to switch your allegiance...to have it cleared by betraying your new allegiance?"

"Will you help us?" The boy breaks through the drama.

"Fuck off, *Prince*!" She snarls at him. "Me helping you is not tying you up and sending you to the gods myself."

I walk closer to Diania, leaving the boy near the door, and I put a hand on her shoulder. "Diania, you owe me."

"I owe nothing!" She releases herself from my grasp.

"'*Nltrueehee*!" It's the Vidicium word for repay. "I am demanding you repay your debt to my wife!"

"You wouldn't dare use her debt for this." She tilts her head.

"But I do dare." I turn and look at the boy, who gives me a confused look. "Diania, repay your end of the bargain."

"Fine!" she concedes. "Fuck, Vesten...your wife may behead you for me for using her debt."

"Aye...Aye, I know."

"Then fine, your debt is repaid. I have a small boat you can use and as for a weapon...well, since you will be dead soon, I guess you deserve this."

She walks around the cluttered smithy, trying her best to scour through the endless amounts of metal and sheaths that cover most floors. Eventually, she sets her sights on a nicely wrapped blade that she hands to me.

"What is this?"

"A sword...I made it a long time ago." She looks down. "You know...*before*."

"You made a sword for Erron?"

"I was going to give it to Amarille to give to him...but since you are using her debt, it's yours."

"I will make sure Amara knows how much you have helped me, and that this debt is more than fulfilled."

"Won't be any use to me sitting around. Took me months to craft, used Amberrock metal so it won't be broken or rust anytime soon. I know you will enjoy the design as well."

"How the fuck did you get Amberrock?" I laugh, amazed.

"By not talking so goddamn much, you old wrinkled-looking shit."

She unveils it. The sword is exceptionally shiny. The special metal she used is whiter than most typical steel blades, causing it to almost look like paper. The hilt of the sword looks typical to most advanced craftsmen, and the real highlight of the weapon is the base and cross guard. Metal designed to look like a fox's head from above, the snout leading into the blade and the ears being the curve of the cross guard. To top it off, there's a slight curve at the very top of the sword, no doubt from the metal being so difficult to work with.

I have never seen this type of metal before in person, only from stories illustrations other ship captains and ship hands have. Some would go as far as to say the scars on their bodies were caused from the lightning that can spring from the metal being swung too fast. Others would say that they had the sword but lost it to fire, which was false for a lot of reasons…not even molten lava could tamper with this blade once forged into a sword.

She presses her finger against the blade. "Spin it fast enough, the blade will glow bright orange. After that, the next attack you do will send a shockwave where it hits."

Diania turns herself away from the blade and searches through a few more piles until pulling out a sheath for the blade. The sheath in and of itself is quite dull compared to the actual blade, more or less a small band that can hold it in place but not cover the beauty of it.

"It's…awesome," the boy chimes in.

"What are you going to name it?" Diania smirks at me.

I look down at the fox, and immediately my mind goes to my wife. I grasp the sword with one hand and feel the weight of it. It's light enough to carry with one hand but has a long enough hilt that using two would be just as viable.

"This was never meant to be my sword….'Erron'," I whisper, putting the scabbard over my side and sheathing the blade.

Diania looks at me for a moment, holding her tongue.

"After all this, we are *just barely* even," she says.

"Thank you, Diania." I reach an arm out to grab hers as a show of respect. "Amarille will know this favour you have done for me, I can promise you that at least."

"Great." She sighs. "Now get the fuck out of my forge."

5

WHAT'S NEXT?

Nothing like being on a small boat with a child you do not know, and if someone finds out either of you, you and your family will be killed from either side. Classic.

The small boat is wonky, splintered, and far too cramped for my liking. The two paddles I opt to just row with myself leave slight splinters on the inside of my palms. The waves are way too high for this small of a ship. Water splashes on the inside, and while that's uncomfortable, it's nothing compared to the young prince's wails.

"The water is too cold," he squeals. "There is no way this is healthy."

"Winter is coming to an end as we approach the south. This is warm compared to usual."

Nevertheless, he clutches himself, trying to remain warm. I just roll my eyes and continue to paddle. Klikia and Summerwind have notoriously warm days matched with extremely cold nights. The water that was once pleasant while the orbs of the day were out is now extremely cold.

"It won't take us too long to get to Olgierdum, just a few more hours at this rate."

"And then what?"

"And then we march for Triumph." I release the paddles and lift them out of the water. The waves can carry us a little farther without manual labor. "The waves are kind to me today."

"To us."

"Sure."

Finally, back to silence and peace, I continue to paddle.

"So you're from here, I presume? Most mercenaries are."

"I am more from Aestas than Klikia now," I say.

"So you are loyal to Slimhixe like the rest of the islands?"

"The islands don't obey anyone except themselves," I snarl. "Hell, most of the guards there are no more loyal than the mercenaries."

"Oh…"

"Does the king really believe that we are loyal to you?"

"Well, they fought for us for hundreds of years." He tilts his head over the boat and looks into his own reflection. "He claims he knows everything."

"I bet he does." I spit off the side. "We used to fight for you back when Verenden was bound under one king, and the only thing we had to fight was poverty…now Summerwind wants the kingdom and, well, it gets complicated."

"Sorry, don't know much outside the words of my father."

"Well, at least for once…you'll know something he doesn't."

He continues to stare over the ship, watching his reflection in the water.

* * *

With a loud thud, I open my eyes, looking around for any sort of land, but there's nothing.

"Boy, wake up!" I demand, watching him jump and wobble the ship.

I look all throughout the water for anything out of the usual and find nothing but the crystal-clear water. Small red eyes form from the bottom and slowly, slowly grow larger.

I fling my head back as fast as I can and draw my sword. "Move your head away, don't look into the water!" I snarl.

"Why?"

"*Ahh no please!*" a voice calls out to us from underneath the water, slowly making its way faster and faster until finding itself above.

"*Please come help me!*"

"Who is it?"

"A Mimicscream. If you stare into it, it will take on the form of someone you love."

"What?" His voice cracks.

I can see his head trying to poke up over the ship to catch a glance at the crying voice. Some form of magic is at play to lure people to their deaths at the bottom of the sea.

"Don't fucking look, Boy!" I scream at him, so he turns his head towards me.

His previous eye color now takes the form of something bright red. His nose is bleeding, and a large, almost uncanny smile takes form on his face. He jumps over the side of the boat, splashing into the freezing water and wailing around as best he can.

I lift my arm over the side of the ship and try to grab onto his collar, just losing him under the still water as he swims towards the voice. I peer into the water only, making sure not to make eye contact with the creature. I turn the boat towards him and begin to row as fast as I can, nearly making it to him. I reach my arm over and grab a hold of his collar, looking down from the top of his head. I can see blood pour from his nose into the frigid ocean.

The cold air is halted, however, with a warm breath just in front of my face. I look up to meet the gaze of Amarille, her bright eyes staring deep at me. I feel my eyes begin to cloud in a thick red smog while my nose begins to drip blood onto the boy's head.

I try my best to pull away but feel like one end of a magnet is pressing against the other side. I'm being forced to bring myself closer and closer.

I try to speak but only blood and ichor spew from my mouth. I begin to choke as my airways slowly fill, all while I see my wife staring at me from the top of the water.

I feel my body lose most of its control, and I fall face first into the deep, black ocean. I try to shake my body as much as I can. I try to release the grasp that looking into the eyes of my wife has on me, but I can't. The shaking of both saltwater and blood filling my lungs is too much before the creature finally swims down to meet my gaze.

Grey skin and long green seaweed for hair, two bulging eyes that seem to be falling out of its skull, and a long horse-like snout. I feel the control over me break, but it's not enough. I attempt to swim higher but feel it pulling my legs farther and farther down.

I kick and scream, watching red blood clouds spray in front of my face in the unbearable water. With a swift tug, I feel myself getting pulled away from the Mimicscream, watching its wide snout open and yell under the water, causing a piercing screech to ring in my ears.

I feel one of my arms breach the black water and feel the wooden splintered boats centre among my fingertips. A hand grasps my forearm and tries to lift myself above the water. I clench the side of the boat, and with the remainder of my strength, feel myself flung out of the water and up into the boat. My lungs feel like they are on fire as I cough up seawater and blood all over the boat.

"Vesten, your sword!" The boy shakes me.

I lift my body up, gasping, and look down towards the blade at my side, previously white but now emitting a bright orange glow as if it is on fire.

"Help us!"

"Help us!"

"Help us!"

Three new Mimicscreams rise from the top of the water. Slowly, they shift their bodies and faces into the shapes of our loved ones. I lean my head down and unsheathe my sword. I make sure not to touch the boy with the blade while I raise it up high into the air. I feel the water underneath the boat course with a few new Mimicscreams that latch their claws into the side of the boat.

"Keep your hands in the boat!" I yell at the boy.

I twist my wrist once and fling the blade down into the water. Bright purple sparks are spraying all around us as the orange disappears with a loud crack. Nothing but screaming and bright purple sparkles fill the water for what seems like a lifetime before everything falls to a deep silence. Back to nothing but the waves and birds creating their natural ambience. A slight sizzle and steam emit from the now white blade I clutch to myself as I lie back into the boat.

"That was...awesome," he says.

I simply roll my eyes and let out a small laugh, still wiping some of the blood out of my nose and spitting blood over the side of the boat. I pick up both of the paddles and continue towards Olgierudum. My arms are now extremely sore and my body frigid basking in the chilled air of the southern nights over the ocean.

It's nights like this when I especially miss being home. Amarille in my mind always emits a warmth like the burning coals of a fireplace. I miss sleeping next to her and smelling her hair. This entire life of fighting and destruction, and all I wanna do is hold her.

Out in the distance, I finally see civilization, bright lights, and when we get closer, some talking. The boat suddenly feels smaller than it did before, now seeing all of the potential leg room and places away from the water in front of us. Once we finally get to the dock, I pull the boat into the pier and hop out of the boat. The prince struggles for a few moments but then finds himself hopping over and onto the pier to meet me. I reach my foot over and kick the boat back into the ocean, maybe to be encountered by more Mimicscreams or to be salvaged for wood to fix ships.

I look around at the small town for anything to tell me where we are so I can get a footing on where to go next. Eventually, I see a large wooden post that reads, "Wicked's Trading." I guess we've found ourselves in a trading port much like Klikia's entire province, only this one doesn't have secret weapons making plans away from any empire.

I look around at a few of the new buildings, now noticing the prince beside me shivering. I figure we should both head to an inn. I finally see a taller building with a wooden plank hovering over the top that reads, "Wicked's Rest."

"Come on," I say, nudging him towards the inn.

We both walk into the inn, past a few drunk people outside singing a few songs, and are met with the piercing smell of sweet alcohol that reminds me of how my ship would usually smell on the lower deck after visiting Summerwind on trade runs. This is an exceptionally crowded inn, the bar on the lower floor busy to the brim with people demanding drinks from the Dragonkin male behind the bar.

I push my way through the crowd of people to reach the front of the bar table as the Dragonkin shuffles his way around washing glasses and then filling them with ale. His green skin is covered in the orange of the peach alcohol while he multitasks as much as he can.

"Another round for us! Dragon!" a female mercenary from behind me slurs.

"Give me more of the peach stuff," a man demands.

I turn around to face the crowd. "Is that a siren?"

I watch most of the crowd turn around and begin to run out of the inn, drawing their swords and jumping onto their ships. I know that any worthwhile trader would kill for a siren head at this time of the year. With inflation it would easily be enough to feed a crew for a few months.

The Dragonkin man turns to see most of the crowd gone, a few stragglers and myself in front of him as he leans onto the desk.

"Where did they go?" His deep voice rings out.

"Siren," I say.

"Really?" He smiles.

"No." I laugh. "I need a room, though. Do you have any?"

"One bed okay?"

"Yeah, I can sleep on the floor, and my son can sleep on the bed."

I toss my hand back to feel my back pocket in search of my coin purse, for a moment completely forgetting that it's probably at the bottom of the ocean with my ship.

He notices me struggling and shrugs his shoulders. "Don't worry about it, families can get by for a debt."

"Thank you kindly, mister."

He reaches down below the desk and hands me a rusted key. I nod my head at him and pull the boy maybe a little too hard by the arm, causing him to jolt. I take him with me to the top room so we can finally put an end to this horrific night. Walking up the crooked wooden stairs and finding our room. Number 22 was engraved onto the door. I push the key in and open it up, basically throwing the boy in and releasing my grasp from him.

I walk inside the room with him. It's nothing fancy. Sloppy woodwork all around, clearly made from people who didn't care. One poorly made bed in the centre, a night table, and a chair next to an open window letting the cool air flow in.

I attempt to walk out and close the door once he is in and settled.

"Wait! Where are you going?"

"Out," I reply, walking towards the door as swiftly as I can.

He slams the door before I can pull it open and I rub my fingers in between my eyes.

"Fucking wait!" he basically cries at me. "I deserve some answers as to what those things were on the boat. I deserve to know why you act as if I don't exist. Who's Amarille? Who's Erron?"

"Boy...mind your tongue. You do not get to speak his name."

"So at least tell me what those things were!"

"They were nothing!" I say to him. "Nothing compared to what will become of our fates if anyone finds out about where we came from and who you are, understand?" He nods his head. "I will be back soon, okay? Just don't die while I am gone, cause if you die then there will be no one left to redeem my family."

I walk out the door and leave him alone in the room, walking back downstairs and seeing the Dragonkin man serving a few new patrons. I walk up to the counter and lean on it, waiting for him to make his rounds before seeing me at the end.

"Can I get you something?" he says.

"There an Inkmaster in this port?"

"Aye, one down the road, looking to get a tattoo?"

"Something like that...thank you again, mister."

I nod, and he does the same. Then I walk away from the inn and out into the port once more. I look towards the ports and piers and notice most of the ships are gone, no doubt after the Siren. My small boat is gone as well, and I laugh thinking to myself what would drive someone to steal something so inconvenient for the weather.

I take a walk down the side of the road, the crisp smell of the end of night and beginning of morning reminding me of Aestas when I would wake up super early to watch the sun rise out on the sea.

I eventually find the Inkmaster, a simple quill dripping ink engraved into a wooden board. I walk in and see a tall elven woman with tattoos all over her body. The building is quite small, enough for one client at a time, with a single chair in a small room. If anyone else wants to get one, they may even have to wait outside. Technically, if business was booming, it could stretch back to the front of the inn.

"Looking for a tattoo?"

"Aye," I say, taking a deep breath and remembering I am not talking to a child. "You accept late payments on ink?"

"Most of the sailors here do late payments." She scoffs as if I should have known. "What of, darling?"

"Two foxes underneath a peach tree and, underneath it, a smaller fox with an E above it."

"You like foxes?"

"Yeah…something like that."

6

CAPTAIN

I wake up on the stone cold floor, my back feeling like it's ten years older than me. I get up and hear a loud crack in my neck that I immediately rub with my fingers. Ow.

I look around the room and feel the blistering heat on my forehead. It must be closer to midday, meaning we are already late on our travels. I try to locate the boy and see him cuddled up next to a pillow covered in sweat and deep in his sleep. I walk over to him and tap him on the head to wake him up, watching him flail and swing his arms at me before coming back to his senses.

"You good?" I ask him.

"Yeah…just had a nightmare, that's all."

"Alright, well let's get a move on, okay? We are already late into our travels."

I can tell from his eyes he does not want to speak. Nor do I truly want to dive more into it.

"Okay."

I help him out of the bed, and we make our way towards the door. Placing one palm against the hilt of my blade and the other on his shoulder to ensure the boy never leaves my sight or gets too far away, we walk down the stairs until reaching the main part of the bar

Only this time, it's a lot more crowded. Hard to even see the Dragonkin man behind the bar as most people swarm around and barely give an inch of elbow room.

The boy, although not short, has no way of seeing past the massive wave of people walking about. I try to make sure my non-sword hand remains on his shoulder to guide him through. A person bumps into me, and we immediately lose contact. I swing my arm around the crowd of people but find no luck in retrieving him.

"Boy?" I call out, immediately realizing my voice doesn't carry enough to pierce through the dense group of people.

I begin to push through a bunch of people, a few of them moving out of the way quite easily and others more like walls than humans. "Out of my way."

I finally make it to the one part of the inn that seems to have a little shoulder room. I turn around to see if I can spot the boy through the thick smog of people who essentially create a wave in their leather armour and rags. All of them gather around one table in the middle, and I imagine someone must be telling quite the story to get this many people interested.

Finally, above the crowd, I see the boy waving his arm. His lighter skin and lack of a tan is a clear outlier from the rest. I walk over to the crowd of people and push them away to get to the front. Moving my arms through them, I eventually find the source of the riveting conversation.

A man I recognize wipes a new scar with a rag dipped in the orange ale. He wears an eyepatch across his face. Looking up at me, his eyes widen, and he stands up and points to me.

"Captain?" Berric calls to me, interrupting his own story.

"Berric?" I chime back to him.

"I thought you perished beneath the waves." He chuckles but not in a way I'm used to. His voice sounds like it's full of molasses.

"Same with you," I say cautiously.

"Please, Captain, take a seat!" He motions with his free hand, the one not covered in alcohol and blood, to the empty chair in front of him. "I was just telling our story."

I do as he says and sit in the chair in front of him, taking my hand away from my blade and resting them both on the table in front of us.

"Please, do not let me interrupt your story. I am just as curious as these folks."

"Aye." He slams his fist into the pitcher of ale next to him and presses the rag once more against his face. "So there I was on the top deck, storms, tornadoes, and the entire might of the gods against us! I look over at some of my crew mates and see them taken from me by the sheer gravity alone. Some of them even breaking their fucking legs as they are slammed into the ground with the changing waves!"

"Aye, the storms wrath was—"

"But then I looked for my captain, to see him running towards the lower deck. I kept thinking over and over and over what could he possibly be getting from there? Our ale?" The bar laughs with him. I feel my hands tense, and suddenly I am aware of where the hilt of my blade is. "That's when, even for a swift moment, I saw our new friend!"

I see the boy restrained by two men behind him with a knife at his throat while the Inn comes to a screeching halt of silence. I attempt to stand up but feel a few men grab my shoulders and arms and fling me back into the chair. My two arms are now held by two seemingly malnourished previous crew mates I only somewhat recognize.

"Berric, let us not do anything any of us might regret. I need the boy alive."

"And why is that? Seeing you now, I have so many questions…why leave the ship, why didn't the almighty *Froh'v* go down with his pride?" He raises an eyebrow. "Who the fuck is the kid?"

"Someone who is going to help Amara," I try to plead. "If he is injured, he will not be able to promise that."

"It always has to do with her, doesn't it?" Berric stands up and draws his axe. Aiming it towards me, he swings his hand over to the boy, slashing him across his face. Blood pours onto the table.

The bar quickly disperses, leaving only the men holding me and the boy, and Berric, the only ones who seem to want any type of conflict.

I fling both of my hands down, releasing myself from their grasp and head-butting one of them as they come close. Freeing my hand, I toss the person to the other crewmate who throws them back to me.

I draw *Erron* from its sheath and grasp it with two hands, pointing it at the three of them gathered around the boy.

"The boy is a simple trader. He comes from nothing. He will not be able to benefit you like he will me!" I try to reason once more.

Berric begins to laugh with his four crew mates holding rusted swords who seem to reluctantly join in.

"You may actually be able to kill me, Captain. But not until I slit this boy's throat if he doesn't tell me who he is and why you have suddenly grown so attached to him."

The boy looks at me, and I shake my head no.

"I am Eli Triumph of Slimhixe…my father is the king!" he screeches, and everyone goes silent.

Berric's face goes from one of shock to one of admiration. Surely, much like myself, he could never have predicted our cargo's level of importance.

"Oh…Captain." Berric laughs. "You are going to wish you went down with the ship after what I do to your new friend here."

The two crewmates slam the prince onto the table in front of us.

The boy gasps as Berric raises his axe in the air. The boy desperately and violently kicks, overpowering the malnourished crew mates, and slides over the table to avoid Berric's axe slamming down into it. He gets up and rushes behind me.

"Now is only the beginning," I snarl.

"For me," Berric snarls back. "Get him, boys!"

Two of the men run towards me and lunge their blades. I push the boy away with my back and deflect the first man's sword, spinning him around with one arm and kicking him in his stomach. He nearly stabs himself in the process with his own blade. The second man seems to be a much better fighter, knowing the basic parry and dodge of someone a bit higher ranking than himself.

I, of course, know the counter. I wait until he slashes overhead and then swing my body around, with one spin I fling his sword away, and with the second and final spin, I slash straight through his chest. *Erron* makes a swift *SHING* as if being sheathed as it cuts him apart like cake.

The other man attempts to get up and swing, but I kick his blade. The rust falls away from the metal and towards the door. I slash across his chest much like his friend before he can say any final words. He falls to the ground, right on top of the other. I look down at my sword and notice the small orange hue glowing from it.

I look over to the two remaining mates next to Berric.

"I offer you two what the others did not have, a chance to escape."

One of the men looks towards the other and then back at Berric before throwing his rusted sword at my feet and attempting to run out the door.

Berric yells and takes his axe above his head, bringing it down with all his force and throwing it into the head of the man who just nearly made it to the door.

The bar is now nothing but for the boy behind me, Berric, and the final crew mate, who lunges at me.

I swing my sword out from underneath me and slam his hands upwards towards the air, causing his blade to point at the ceiling before spinning and slicing his hand clean off. One of his hands is still throbbing and clutching onto the sword as blood spews from the top of it. Berric simply laughs and grabs his axe out of the poor lad's head.

"One last chance, Berric. For old times' sake, just walk away."

"You know, Captain? Some of us actually like going down with the ship. Some of us actually like dying with honour."

"Honour is an unknown word to you," I snarl.

"Much like the word widow will become apparent to your wife!"

He slashes away at me, his brute force and anger anticipated but more than I expected. I try to spin but instead find all of my stamina drained with the simple act of blocking his enraged swings. Ducking over a side swing, I watch him take a piece of the wall out while the boy runs out the door.

With just the two of us in the middle of an empty inn, I try and take the offence for once, striking him before he can strike me. He clasps the bit of my sword into the curve of his axe and punches me directly in the nose. My sword finally detaches and slides away from his axe, blood pouring down to the floor from my clearly broken nose.

I've never actually fought him before. Sure, we practiced a few times with wooden swords, but you can never determine a person's grit from sparring. Only how much they truly care about keeping the bones in your hands intact. He's a lot stronger than I am, far more than any other fighter I have ever faced. I know if he throws me off my feet, I will die with one swing if I am unable to block with my entire body behind it.

"That is a lovely sword," he snarls. "Wonder if I'll use it to kill the prince and dismember your hand to send back to Amara."

"Do not speak her name!" I swing at him while he laughs, and he uses my anger against me by parrying away with his body and slamming me down.

I attempt to get up but see him stand over me, lifting the axe high into the air and bringing it directly down for my skull. I know I won't be able to deflect all of it with a simple raise of my blade, but I do it anyway in hopes of a miracle. His metal blade slams into my bright orange one as a loud thunderous crack erupts, and purple streaks of lighting emit from the whitish silver.

He gets hit directly in the chest by a large bolt of purple energy and flies across the room, hitting his back against the wooden wall, splintering it in the process before falling onto his back. He coughs up blood and attempts to lift his arm and axe, but I walk over unfazed and kick his weapon away. *Erron* is now back to its typical white steel. I raise it over his head.

"Wait! Wait!" He coughs and wheezes. "Amara would not be proud of you!" He coughs up some blood.

"Don't invoke her name, you son of a bitch," I snarl and swing my blade down into his throat. The steel tears away at his neck.

I look around the now completely silent room and hear some slight whimpering from behind the bar. I walk over to find the source of the noise and see the Dragonkin man in the fetal position with his scaly tail between his legs.

"Are you okay?" I ask him, trying to extend a hand, but he swipes it away.

"Get out! Get out! Please!" he screeches.

I take a deep breath and nod. Then I sheath my blade and pick up Berric's axe, which I'll no doubt be able to sell for a good bit of profit.

"Sorry for the trouble, mister." I walk out of his inn and see the boy among a group of civilians who avoid him like a plague. "Come on, Boy."

He walks over to me, and I grab his arm forcefully, bringing him with me. Our walk to the next town over will take a while on foot, but hopefully while we are there, we can find a horse of some kind. We won't survive long without faster means of travel and better capacity for food storage than the rucksack around the boy's back, which I do not question how he acquired.

"Ever tell people you're the prince again, I will temper my sword into your heart, understand?"

"Yes, Fox."

"Ever call me Fox again, and I will slit your throat." I sigh. He smiles slightly at me before we leave the pier as swift as possible and make our way along the main road. "Where did you get that rucksack?"

"Found it." He smiles. "Can I use the axe since you have a sword?"

"No."

7

SOFTSAND & SORE FEET

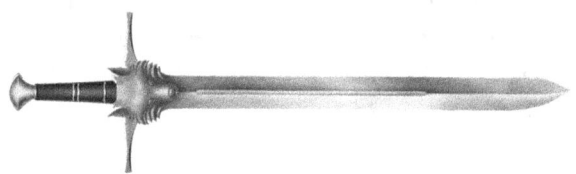

We walk through the blistering heat which, the longer we stay in, the more I realize how much I despise. Heat is terrible to control in the regulation of human temperature. In the cold, you can put an extra layer on and stay close to a fireplace, but in the heat your options are as sparse as the water you carry.

Following the main path and hoping to avoid the sight and contact of any royal legion from either side is no small feat. Nevertheless, a man wielding a sword walks with a prince.

"So we are wanted now?"

"Aye, by both sides."

"How long until both sides find out about us?"

"I imagine it will take a while to pass on the message. They'll have to send a raven to each town, but that is after they get it decreed by a diplomatic person of power."

The boy shakes his head, as if he is amazed at my answer.

"How did you know that?" He looks up at me.

"My wife used to be a diplomat for Slimhixe. If we were still on that side of the war, she probably would have been the person to sign off on it."

"Why aren't you anymore?" He stops and looks at me.

I stop as well, eyeing him up and down in an attempt to see his endgame. "Conflicting interests."

"Cryptic." He smiles. We continue walking. "Next town is Softsand, did you know that?"

"No."

"Awesome," he says.

"Why is that awesome?" I scoff.

"It means you need me just as much as I need you. You can use the sword, and I will be...the diplomat, just like your wife!"

"Did you just compare yourself to my wife, Boy?"

He immediately looks as if he has somehow drawn a knife to me, realizing the error of his phrasing. He goes back to traversing silently throughout the grass and sand.

"You know...you can call me Eli," he says to break the silence. "If you want."

I guess it never occurred to me I've been calling him anything other than his name. I suppose that goes to show the lack of connection I try to associate with new people. Especially those of rivalling empires and one so high up in the royal bloodline, of all things.

"Alright...Eli," I say, watching him smile. "Is there some type of Trader at Softsand?"

"It's a pretty run of the mill town. I only ever visited once or twice while Father went on his diplomatic run of power. Now, I actually think it belongs to Summerwind."

"Wait...his diplomatic what now?"

"You know...where he goes town to town to show his power and all that?"

"Never knew a king that was so anxious to demand power. Power should be implied not demanded."

"Oh...I guess you're right."

"I guess with Summerwind rising closer to power, your father is trying all of his luck."

"I guess so." Eli goes quiet.

We go back to walking awkwardly and alone throughout the path.

Finally, we seem to be getting close to Softsand. More and more traders on horses and carriages are making their way out to some of the farms that reside on the outskirts of the town. Luckily for us, Softsand was essentially nulled due to Olgierdum being more or less a peaceful province. Always a battle between the two sides, it never seemed to be anything more than a middle ground battlefield.

Olgierdum became quick to host thieves, marauders, and mercenaries hiding under the gaze of both empires that never wanted to reach far enough out to deploy any type of law.

Out in the distance, I see Softsand, up a hill from the farms and typical peasantry. It was actually rather lavish. Tall walls, high end buildings, and a seemingly booming population, despite being a technical forefront desired capture of the war.

We walk casually. My feet and legs are sore, and I cannot wait to find a place to rest for the night. We must have been walking for hours upon hours, and no doubt before long it will be back to a painfully cold night. No doubt warmer from fires throughout the city compared to the chilled salt water.

Finally making our way into the town, we see it's mostly Elves, most of them in higher-end fabrics and an abundance of Summerwind guards, which explains the lavishness. I take a look around at the entrance and try to follow signs and the commotion of people to find points of interest.

"Huh," I say.

"What?"

"High-end place for being in Olgierdum."

An inn smack dab in the middle of everything will be a good place to rest later in the evening once we've accomplished our tasks. I see Eli eyeing a few of the girls from across the road towards the brothel and elbow him in the side.

"Ow," he exclaims, perhaps a bit too exaggerated.

"Focus, we have things to accomplish. Now help me find a shop."

"There!" He wastes no time. I am not sure if he was trying to be extra quick in order to prove his own worth to me. "Just in front of the brothel…see I am focused."

I just sigh and watch Eli take the lead to the shop and try to slyly move himself towards the women and men all dancing around the bathhouse. I grab him by the shirt and move him over. Having him open the door to the shop, I turn around to smile at the group of people who laugh, no doubt thinking a father is trying to control his teenage son.

The shop is high-end like most you'd find in the city half of Summerwind's province. It's cooled with an ice pit at the side, which radiates frost. There are weapons that looked fancy, as if meant to hang in a home as opposed to using them to fight. Clothing that mainly consists of thin linen for the heat, and of course, random Elven jewelry scattered about.

I walk up to the Elven woman running the shop and notice her uniquely purple hair tied up into a ponytail. Her purple eyes match her hair, and her thin linen dress the same as the one on display.

"How may I help you two, gentlemen?"

"Looking to sell," I say as nice and compassionate as I can while also lugging the axe onto the table. "It is steel from Dulacas. A province on The Islands."

"Seems sloppy," she scoffs.

"Never said Dulacas was any good, ma'am." I laugh. "Used to belong to a friend. Used it for nearly as many years as I have been alive."

"So a short amount of time?" She eyes my reddish hair.

"You flatter me." I twist the wedding ring on my finger, watching her de-tense her body. "Interested in buying or shall I find a smithy?"

"May I?" She reaches her hands out, her purple nails matching the rest of her aesthetic.

I slide it closer to her, respecting her courtesy as best I can.

She lifts it up and inspects it, dragging her palm across the blade end to assure it is still sharp and clutching the hilt in her palm while twisting the wrist to check the weight.

"So?" Eli now slides his way into the conversation, walking in front of me and leaning across the table with one hand. I wonder if I'm trying to impress the Elven woman, who stares down at him.

"I can do 100 gold pieces. Consider it a favour for you and your son here." She smiles down at him and then meets my gaze once more. "Deal?"

"Aye." I nod my head. "Thank you, ma'am."

She nods back and reaches down underneath her table. I hear the sound of clinking metal before she pulls up a brown coin purse with an ink engraving of 100.

"No need to count," I assure. "I trust." I nod at her.

"Have a good evening, you two! And Brenuin's blessings!"

Just before I walk out of the shop after pulling at Eli's collar so he leaves the shopkeeper alone, I notice a small black leather-bound book with a small slot along the spine for a quill and ink. I lift it up in my hands and walk back towards the purple adorned shopkeeper.

"How much?" I ask her.

"Five gold pieces." She smiles. "Are you an artist or someone who likes letters?"

"Any chance I can be both?" I smile back, removing the five cold pieces and putting an extra on the table. "Brenuin's blessings!"

I tuck the small book into the coin purse, watching it stick up slightly from the top. Then we make our way back out into the town where shadows now cast over more and more, meaning night will soon be upon us. We will have to be quick for the rest of our adventures.

Eli, of course, goes back to looking at the dancing girls.

"Would the little lord care for a dance?" one of the paler skinned girls chimes to him.

"Well actually I am a pri—"

"Very busy, sadly," I interrupt and grab him by the collar once more to move him throughout the town. "I still mean that thing about tempering my blade into your heart if you announce to someone your upbringing."

I push him slightly so he stumbles and hopefully starts thinking more clearly when speaking to strangers. I bet all his life he was able to tell people he was a prince and have people, weapons, and praise latching themselves in order to get a spot in the royal bloodline that rules over Verenden. Only difference now is with a war, the only thing that will latch to his true self is a sword or pike.

We make our way to a marketplace where I walk up to a man selling bread, rucksacks, and pouches. An odd combination, but it will do just fine. I buy a few pouches and a belt to swing over my side and not have to carry the coin purse in my hand anymore. I buy some bread from him and peach ale from the woman selling next to him. I walk over to Eli and place the food and drink into his bag as he stares at some of the infrastructure of the town.

"What catches your eye?" I ask.

"This place looks a lot…prettier than Slimhixe."

"Yeah well…Slimhixe hasn't exactly had the best run of architecture when they are too busy enforcing shit laws."

"What's that supposed to mean—"

"Come on, boy." I tilt my head towards the inn we saw earlier in the centre of the town and make sure, like always, that the young prince walks in front of me so he doesn't wander off. We walk in and, like in most inns, the deep, rich smell of alcohol pierces our nostrils.

An Elven woman runs the entire thing. The bar section is close to empty. Most elves are not notorious drinkers, unless they're also sailors, I suppose. She has long, blonde hair all the way down to the small of her back and bright blue eyes. She is built strong like a soldier and, through the thin linen of her dress, you can see the outline of her muscles.

I walk through the empty bar and lean over the table, the boy quickly following suit as if to try and mirror my actions.

"What can I get you two?" she asks while cleaning out some wooden tankards.

"Just a room," I say.

"Eight gold pieces for the night." She smiles. "Do not get a lot of humans around these parts."

"Happy to be in the minority." I return her smile and pass the eight gold pieces over.

She turns around and grabs a few keys, sorting through them and passing me one.

"First room on the right up the stairs," she says. "Have a good night you two."

"Cheers."

The boy and I go straight up the stairs and into the room. This one is a lot fancier than the few we visited before. It has thin cashmere sheets and architecture that's flawless down to the last board in the wooden floor. The boy sits on the bed, and I move to the window, sitting on a chair wrapped in firm pillow-like things that make it exceptionally comfortable on my back and sore legs.

The boy is quick to go straight to sleep, removing his rucksack and lying down and almost immediately snoring.

I just sit on the comfortable chair and look out the open window. The cool breeze coming in is exceptionally lovely. I slide my new journal out from my coin purse and remove the ink vial, dipping the quill back in and covering the vial so it does not leak onto the white pages.

I bring the pages up to my nose and smell them. A sweet and musky aroma. I flip the pages all the way until the end. I remember making fun of Amarille for always smelling every new book she got. Being away from her now, the once funny task feels…sad. It's not the same without her making a snarky comment about how she brought me into loving it.

I flip the book open to the first page and begin to draw her face. The freckles and bright eyes I'll have to settle on making black until I can buy coloured ink. I used to draw her quite a bit; in fact it was one of the first times she actually let me see her naked. When we were young teenagers, probably the same age as the prince, we went into a sauna after escaping her father's hounds. My hands that were covered in black ink that left marks on the sides of her cheeks as I kissed her. The sauna we went into for safety was scorching, and it wasn't long before she asked me to draw her.

If I close my eyes, I can still see her. Everything. Her laugh, which usually always ends up evolving into a snort, her bright red hair, her individual freckles, and how, for those few moments when she would bring me into a hug, I knew nothing else would ever make me feel as important as those few seconds. No one else matters except her. That famous night was also the first time she muttered the now famous, "Everything we do, we do for the advancement of ourselves." A line which has become just as famous as the cryptic foxes, one that's been in my family for generations.

I press the ink gently a few times, making the freckles of her face come to life on the paper, finding myself getting lost in memories of her. Getting lost in the drawings of her, as one memory after another, I remember my wife.

"Soon I will be back to you," I whisper.

8

WANTED

I wake up on the padded seat, easily a welcome change in pace from the typical wooden chair or floor setups I hope to never become accustomed to. Eli has already woken up and seems to be staring out the window to my side, sitting on a small pillow on the floor and watching the orbs shine their lights over the Softsand.

I rub my eyes and stand up.

"You talk in your sleep." He breaks the silence. "About people, things, places, everything it seems. Then...nothing."

"Yeah, well...got a lot on my mind, I suppose." I reach an arm out to help him up. "Ready to get a move on?"

"Yeah...let's go."

He reaches up and clasps my arm, lifting himself onto his two feet. We walk together out the door and down the staircase. The summer beams shoot their way through some of the open windows, nearly blinding us as we finally make it to the bottom of the inn. Only, everything feels wrong.

People stare at us, more than anyone should normally stare at a supposed father and son duo simply making their way through the town. I try to look around the room for a reason. We're both still wearing clothing, and my blade is pure white without a tint of fresh blood on it.

"Vesten..." Eli looks over to our side towards the Elven woman staring at us. Behind her, a large poster of a poorly drawn rendition of Eli and me reads 'Wanted: Treason on Both Sides With A Reward of 10,000 Gold'.

"Fuck," I mumble to myself. Then I take Eli by the hand, and we make our way out into the blistering heat.

We hope to escape the mass of people who know we're wanted. However, there are more posters outside than anywhere else. Even some guards put up fresh ones with a rolling pin. Across the street, some of the women from the brothel are even talking to two heavily armoured men donning the Summerwind sigil, their weapons sheathed. Just off to the side of them, I even see the purple haired Elven woman speaking to a guard, motioning some things with her hands before pointing over at the inn.

I grab the boy by the collar and basically slam him into the side of the homes with me, hoping to avoid any contact with anyone else aside from each other.

"I thought you said it would take a while for us to become wanted?" Eli hisses.

"Well, I guess a missing prince and mercenary are higher up than I thought on priority...and the person taking over my wife's job is a lot better than her."

"So what is the plan?"

"We need a disguise of some sort, then we make for the gate leading towards the centre of Olgierdum where there won't be nearly as many guards from either side."

I peek my head out until coming across a merchant stall with thin scarves that should be enough to cover our faces. "Follow me and stick close."

I grab a coin from the small leather purse at my side and throw it just in front of the man watching the stall. His eyes widen, and he walks a few feet away from his stall just long enough for me to snag two scarves for me and the boy. Then we run away and finally make it to the side of two different homes farther away from the guards and people that have seen our faces.

"Cover your face," I say quickly.

I fling the scarf around my neck and over my mouth and nose, leaving just my eyes and hair exposed, then watch Eli do the same.

He looks up at me. "I am ready, let's go."

I grab his hand and walk with him as casually as I can towards the back of the town where the gate will be hopefully open like the one in the front. Trying our best to avoid getting close to any of the posters, we walk through the awfully long town, past home after home that look incredibly close to one another. We finally make it to the back gate. It's closed shut with one guard standing at a lever and the other way off to the side chatting to some locals.

I know this is our only way out, and I know we have to get to the lever. I just don't know how.

"Help!" Eli leaves my grasp and runs towards the guard at the lever. "There is a Griffin on the other side of the town!"

He basically latches to the guard as if the shiny armour is covered in a thick glue. Only the guard doesn't move and instead laughs.

"Nice try, little man, no Griffins this far south."

"Oh…well I am…pretty sure I saw one?" He tries to continue his story. "Oh no wait, it was over there!"

He points his finger to the other side of the guard and the taller man turns his body away from Eli. I watch Eli struggle to think of something before slamming his heel into the back leg of him. The guard lets out a screech and falls on both knees, trying to reach for his sword. Eli grabs the man's helmet and tears it off, spinning and attempting to fling it into the side of his head to knock the man out. However, he spins too fast without spotting his vision on one thing, so he gets dizzy and falls onto his side. Now he holds the man's helmet as the man stands towing over him.

"Bad decision, little man," he snarls.

I run as fast as I can to the man and kick the side of his body before he can draw his sword. He flies farther away than I expected and hits the stone wall next to the gate.

"Halt!" I hear a deeper voice to our side and the unsheathing hiss of a blade.

"Was this your fucking plan?" I snarl at the boy and help him up.

"It went a lot better in my head!"

"In your head there are Griffins this far south, and you know how to spin?"

I run over to the lever and kick it down, watching the gate slowly rise up. Then I raise my hands above my head while pressing Eli and my back against the opening gate.

"Freeze you two!" the one with a sword drawn demands while the other goes beside his comrade and draws his sword.

"Major misunderstanding," I try to reason as the gate is nearly done raising behind us. "You see—"

I hear the click sound of the gate at full mast and grab Eli's hand, running with him as fast as I can away from the gate towards the farmland at the divide of Olgierdum and Summerwind. The clanging metal armour behind us is no match for our lesser clothing and basically lack of shoes on the sand and grass. Soon we're far enough away that we know they'll have to get horses in order to catch up with us.

I take a look at the large variety of farms and settle on the one with an overabundance of horses walking around on an open field. Eli and I run into a large red barn, closing the doors behind us. We take a minute and gasp for air, my heart feeling as if it is beating out of my chest, and my lungs on fire. The boy lets out a loud cough and wipes the sweat from his forehead, removing his scarf.

I turn around to see horses all in individual stables, different breeds and builds, all slamming their hooves into the ground and neighing loudly at the two new intruders.

"Hands up!" I hear a crackly older man's voice call out from the shadows at the end of the dimly lit barn. I reach down to draw *Erron* from its sheath, but just beside my head a large arrow impales the wood with a loud crack. "I don't like asking twice."

I raise my hands and see a somewhat older man, probably around the age of my father, walk out into the light. The wrinkles under his eyes create small pockets that seem to catch the sweat from his brow. His wooden bow looks mangled and nearly half-rotted away, yet he pulls it back with all his might. His form is improper, and I think about Amarille who would insult this man for betraying such an elegant weapon. His arms shake at the mere act of locking the arrow at draw.

"Sir...we do not mean any trouble," I try to reason with both my hands in the air. "My son and I just need to purchase a horse is all."

"They ain't for sale...sir."

"So perhaps an exchange?" Eli chimes in. "Is there anything you require other than money?"

The man lowers his bow slightly and looks off to the side, shaking his head and then drawing it back at us.

"Nothing you two can provide," he scoffs.

"Try us...after all, we are the ones at your mercy, right?" Eli is a far better negotiator when spinning isn't involved.

"My daughter and son...taken early in the night by some guards, they were."

He lowers the bow and throws it off to the side. "Bring them back, and you can take a weak horse."

Well, that was rather easy...maybe I should try being more diplomatic like the naive prince.

"Just...like that?" I ask. "No catch? No more drawing of the bow there?"

"If you two wanted me dead, it would have happened by now... most that come around here don't try to reason...only to fight."

"Thank you, sir," Eli says.

"Come into my home, much brighter in there." He hobbles his way. His voice still sounds as if he's trying to be menacing with the cracks in his tone. "Not much to do in this barn except scoop horse shit, anyhow."

I let the man take the lead and open the barn door for him. Eli raises his arms out in front of him as if to say he's just as surprised at this man's intense need for help and diplomacy as us. We follow him into his small home, no bigger than the barn, with three beds all laid out cramping the small kitchen that also acts as a living area.

"Anyone care for some tea?" the old man calls out, and we both shake our heads no. "Very well."

"I hate to intrude on your hospitality." Eli goes back to being the main talker. "Where exactly *are* your son and daughter?"

"East towards a camp, at least that's what one of the people kept saying to them."

"Wait," I join in. "What exactly did these men say to them?"

"They would be shackled and shared was, I think, their exact words." He looks down at the kettle filled with overflowing black tea leaves.

"That doesn't sound like any guards I know," I say.

"What are you implying?" Eli turns to me.

I lean down to him to whisper. "I think the people who took his family are marauders who stole the armour of guards. Summerwind is not a vagabond group like Slimhixe."

"We will go East first light tomorrow, sir." Eli wastes no time volunteering our service. "We will bring back your family."

I watch the older man sniffle and try to wipe away some tear drops to prevent them from falling into his tea. "Thank you two. Feel free to take whatever food you need."

"Unnecessary, just came from the town."

"Well, feel free to sleep in the stables if you don't mind."

"Actually—" I try to chime.

"We do not." Eli overtakes the conversation and pulls on my hand to bring me outside into the heat and towards the barn. "Do *not* ask to sleep in his missing children bed, Vesten, fucking hells."

"Very well, Boy."

"Shut up."

I like this new meaner Eli.

* * *

ONCE NIGHT HAS FALLEN, Eli seems to have already passed out, despite the constant stream of noises coming from all sides with the horses. I, however, just stare up at the ceiling. I close my eyes and try to think how seemingly unnecessary this entire circumstance is becoming. My wife is on the other end of Verenden, pregnant, while I escort a mere child across the damn country. Gods be good, I will probably see my son by the time he has his first child at this rate.

I remember being at home when Amarille had to leave for business expenditures. I remember how our bed never quite felt as comfortable or right as when she was in it. Even now, it feels wrong to sleep in so many places without being able to turn over and see her face. Alas...I know the faster I complete these minimal tasks, the faster I can get back to that bed. So, I let myself drift off into a peaceful sleep while trying to mute out the sounds of the horses on all sides.

"Vesten." The snoring prince seems to have woken up, and I don't notice because he sounds so similar to the damned horses. "Are you still awake?"

"Aye," I groan, not wanting to walk. "What is it?"

"Thanks for, you know...not killing the old man."

"What?"

"I mean...it seems like you just constantly kill things or backstab for money and stuff. I am glad you didn't kill him and steal a horse. I am proud of you."

He and I both laugh into the darkness.

"Oh? You are proud of me now, are you?"

"Whatever keeps less blood off of that shiny white sword seems like a win for me."

"It would seem like a win for me if the only noises I had to deal with in this barn were from farm animals."

Finally, I'm back to the peace and quiet of simple horses. "Goodnight Vesten."

Gods fucking help me.

"Are you fucking serious, Boy? We are not on a goodnight basis!" I whisper angrily at him, listening to him near-cry of laughter. "Fucking goodnight. I'll show you a goodnight by plunging my sword into your throat."

9

FAMILY BURDENS

"The house looks lovely." Amarilles' voice is just as sweet as it was authoritative.

"It's coming together as best as it could, considering we are building up on the steepest hill imaginable."

"Must you always be so negative?"

I look over towards her. Her bright green eyes reflect the orbs from out in the sea as dusk and shadows slowly cast over us. The orange from the orbs casts over onto her red hair. Hers was always a lot more beautiful than mine. My hair is rusted red like a poorly kept sword that has seen more saltwater than it has blood. Hers, however, is more colourful than the orbs themselves. Any more reddish or orange and it would surely erupt into flames.

"Come here," I whisper.

Reaching my arms out for a hug, I bring her in close for an embrace, wrapping my arms tightly around her waist and leaning my head down into the small part of her neck, my warm breath in the winter air being sent back at me from her cool skin. I take a breath and smell the peach scent that usually comes from her hair, something that reminds us of home in Klikia and Summerwind.

I move away from her and slide my fingers through her hair,

pressing it behind her ears and staring at her smile. Only she isn't smiling. Her mouth slowly leaks out a few small droplets of blood, and before long a small stream of it oozes from her mouth as her eyes portray horror and confusion.

She reaches a hand up to my face and slides blood all across my pale skin. I grab her hand and look down towards her stomach. Her pregnant belly oozes blood. I try to remove my hands from her face and apply pressure to it. I follow her body as she falls to the snowy ground, which now takes on a deep shade of red.

"Beware the red rain, Vesten," she whispers.

"Amara?" I scream at her, trying my best to apply pressure to the open gashes on her stomach. Watching her eyes slowly close and blood-red tears streaming down her face before the last few breaths of life leave her body, and she becomes dead weight.

"Dad?" I hear a voice call out from behind me.

I turn around to see Erron, his long winter robes and bright green eyes staring at me. His hair matches that of his mother, who lays dead underneath me.

"Erron?" I whisper, crying out to him. "Son, look away!"

"Why couldn't you save her?" He rolls up his sleeve revealing the fire quirk tattoo. "Why couldn't you save me?"

I watch as his robes slowly begin to smoke a thick black smog from the fabric.

"Erron!" I run towards him, watching Amarille fade into smoke as I run through her attempting to reach my son. It starts to rain red with such force that it blinds my eyes as I push through to reach him.

Just before I reach him, he is met with a bright flash and screams while being lit on fire. I hear the sound of his boiling flesh as his hand reaches out to try and grab me before he slowly fades into the smog. The black smoke and blood rain surround me until there is nothing... nothing but darkness.

"ERRON!" I yell as loud as I can, drawing my sword and holding it in front of my now-upright body. The barn is quiet but not silent. The horses continue to be on their way while Eli looks over at me.

"Vesten...It's me, Eli...you know me, right?" He moves away from me.

My entire face and body are covered in a cold sweat. It was simply a nightmare, yet everything felt so incredibly real. I even wipe away my own sweat to check if it's the bloody rain. I toss my sword to the side and rub my eyes. I know Amarille was nowhere near pregnant when that house was built, and yet it felt real. I know it was all a nightmare, and yet I felt like a helpless spectator.

"I know who you are, boy. I am sorry."

"Are you okay? Who is Erron?"

"Let's get a move on."

I get up and waste no time gathering my things and walking out of the barn into the heat. My eyes take a quick second to adjust as the orbs pierce their light into the darkened barn. Eli soon follows suit and meets me outside, looking at me, but not before I move on and have him follow close behind.

"Are you not gonna talk about that?" He jogs to keep up with my pace as we head East.

"Nothing to discuss," I reply coldly.

"What do you mean nothing to discuss? You woke up yelling the name of your sword and nearly slashed me."

"I did not nearly slash you."

"Just . . ." He runs up and stops right in front of me. "Fucking wait, we can take a break, you know? I know it seems like time is an enemy, but we can take a day to relax if we need."

"The longer we stay here, Boy, the farther away that man's family gets, and the less of a chance we have to bring his daughter and son back in one piece."

I walk past him, and we continue on our way, slowing my pace so as to not tire him out as we walk East out into the mix of forestry and desert sand: trees that stretch all along in a forest but sand and grass competing for territory wherever possible.

It isn't hard to imagine how The Forest section of the Summerwind can be so lush and green when even this far north of the province, green tries to sneak its way into control.

We walk for what seems like an hour or three, until eventually, while walking in the deep forest that seems to find no end, we end up seeing a small bit of smoke out in the distance. There wouldn't be any true guards out this far East at this time deciding to light a fire unless they are cooking some food they found along the way.

"Alright here is the plan, Boy." I stop walking and lean down towards Eli. "I will bring you up, and you will pretend to be my hostage."

"What, no? I am not going to pretend—"

"Eli, please. If this crowd is planning to do to those people what I believe they are...seeing you out and free would only bring you more harm, understand?"

He takes a minute to think about what I just said. Trying to think of some way to argue before lowering his head and nodding. Flinging his rucksack over his shoulder, he pulls out a small bit of string and passes it over to me while putting his rucksack back onto his back and reaching his arms out.

I tie them slightly harder than comfortable with a typical sailor's knot, usually used for stringing sails up in the ship.

"Ow."

"Alright...let me do all of the talking, okay?" I say. "I have dealt with this type of crowd before and sadly...it usually doesn't end diplomatically as you seem to favor."

"Okay," he whispers.

I take Eli and put him directly in front of me, pushing him slightly with my hand before unsheathing my sword and using the hilt of that to 'gently' move him forward. We make our way faster towards the smoke until, eventually, we see the bright orange pit in the distance surrounded by four guards and two people tied to a tree off to the side. It baffles me that they would leave their hostages so out in the open while also having a fireplace lit during one of the hottest times of the year.

Slowly, I make my way up towards them, catching their attention as I push Eli more and more harshly.

"Aye, who the fuck are you?" one of them snarls.

"Just passing through." I point towards the hostages with my blade. "I see we are all in the same profession."

"We are the king's men," the female one snarls. "You may address us with a little more respect."

"Aye, of course, that is my bad, friends." I throw Eli over towards the hostages. "Wait there."

I walk around the campfire to make my way in front of the four and stab my shiny blade into the sand right next to me. It glows slightly before dispersing as I stop moving it around so much.

"Fancy blade," one of the more silent ones chirps into the conversation. "Where did ya get it?"

"Found it on a corpse on the ocean floor while free diving."

I reach over and take some of the cooking rabbit from the centre and take a large bite into it, watching a few of them grit their teeth.

"Didn't your parents ever teach ya not to steal the authorities' food?"

"Aye," I say, looking over to Eli as he goes behind the tree of hostages and tries to free his hands. "And you are all the good service of the king's men…what exactly is your code of honour?"

"What do you mean?" the girl chirps up.

"When you are knighted, you are sworn by eternal blood and all that nonsense…do you all remember it?"

They all look at each other and nod their heads one after another. I notice, as they nod, some of the armour flings to the side of their shoulders instead of being perfectly fitted as it would for any other normal member of the king's service.

"Funny," I reply, taking another bite from the steaming hot meat.

"Why is that funny?" the first man asks, tilting his head.

"I used to know quite a few guards…" I throw the rabbit into the sand. "And they never did mention a code of honour."

I watch one of their eyes widen before I stand and fling my sword out from the sand with a loud hiss. I kick the mix of sand and food scraps from the fire towards the man just across from me and dive over to my right just behind a log. Leaping into a roll and then spinning the blade with both my hands, I decapitate the first man.

The woman and two other men all stand up and draw their blades. I notice their sloppy footwork as they can barely move in armour too tight or too big for their respective sizes. My sword is already glowing bright orange. I wait for all three to attack before deflecting all of their steel with my blade. Sliding my blade quickly down the woman's sword before cutting her hand, I go into a spin, slashing her and the other three all at once. With the final bit of the sword hitting the third one's body, the blade erupts with its common thunderous crack, and all three of them fly backwards towards the hostages and Eli, who finally manages to remove himself from the bounds.

Pieces of armour are now flung off while two of the fabled king's service lie dead on the ground, and the quieter man stands up hobbling with his sword.

"What the fuck was that?" He spits blood out onto the ground. "Didn't know you had a quirk?"

"Didn't know stealing armour meant free will to take a person's family," I starkly reply.

Eli looks over towards the back of the man.

"Vesten, look out!" he yells.

Just as I look towards Eli, I see the man in front of me draw a small crossbow from his back and fire, not impaling me but slashing away at my chest and lodging itself into the tree behind me. I run over and stab the man in his chest, then stand there watching him cough up blood and fall onto his back.

I fall back onto the log as Eli gets to work unbinding the hostages. I press my hand against my chest and feel the warm blood mixed with sweat on my palm.

Eli removes the two people's binds and the gags from their mouths.

"Thank you," the older blonde sibling calls out before looking at me. I try to cover my bleeding. "Lyra, go help him!" She rushes over and leans me back onto the log.

"I am alright—" I cough up some phlegm and blood. "Just a scratch really."

"That is definitely not just a scratch…mister?"

"Vesten," I reply to the girl and guy while Eli walks over the bodies of the guards.

"Janun! Go see if any of them have any medicine to combat infection!" she demands of her sibling.

"I do not know what to look for," he replies anxiously.

"Just look for a fucking box or something with a life quirk symbol on it!"

I watch him run out of my view, and then I stare up at the girl's torn up rags. I guess I got to her too late before a few of them had already slashed at her with, I imagine, some pointed sticks. I note a few cuts along her face as well, and I imagine her brother shares a lot of the same wounds.

"Got it!" Janun runs back over to me and hands her a box.

"Yes! Brilliant!" She pulls out a brownish green vial and removes the cork with her teeth. She is just about to pour before lifting up my gambeson and shoving parts of it into my mouth. "This is going to hurt. I am sorry."

She wastes no time before pouring the liquid onto my skin and over the wound. A rush of pain ensues. It feels like my chest has been shoved into burning coals of a fireplace. I'm reminded of when I was younger and bloodied by some dogs of a rival mercenary.

"Ah, fuck!" I scream.

"Is he going to be okay?" I hear Eli's voice but cannot place him anywhere.

Eventually the burning sensation stops, and instead I am left with an intense throbbing sensation mixed with a feeling of ice cold. The polar opposite of what I first experienced when she poured that ghastly liquid into my exposed side.

"I have dealt with the worst…on horses—but still." She removes a sewing kit and begins to get to work on repairing the open gash bleeding onto the side of the log. I feel slight pinches of pain as she moves the thread and needle in between my skin and pulls deeply until, eventually, she is finally done. "Help me get him up, Brother."

The two siblings lift me up and onto my feet. I fling my gambeson back over that section of my chest, careful not to apply pressure to it. I lean over, feeling the pain shoot up my side, and sheathe my sword after wiping some of the blood onto my pants.

"Thank you kindly," I groan to her.

"Well, you did just save us, so consider us even." Janun reaches over and puts a hand on my shoulder. "You were here to save us, right?"

I nod at them and look over at Eli, who is lifting up one of the dead bandit's swords.

"Eli, what are you doing?"

"Taking a sword."

"No, fucking hells, do not take one of those swords. It would not be weighted properly to you and you would have no place to keep it."

"But I—"

"Put down the sword, you little fuck," I yell.

"Is he your son?" Lyra asks.

"Gods help me if he was."

10

OLGIERDUM INTO OLGIERDS RUM

"How is your leg?"

"Can you walk?"

The siblings continuously berate me with increasing questions. I mean, I understand I saved them from certain fate, but I was expecting a bit more…peace. Yes, there is now a slight hobble to my walk, which reminds me of my aged father, but I'm still just as nimble as ever. So long as I do not end up fighting someone short enough to try and stab my legs off.

Eli is uncharacteristically quiet. I'm not sure if maybe it's because I told him he couldn't keep a sword, but all I can say about the matter is…thank god. I finally remember what the voice inside my head feels like. I'm very particular about the company I keep around myself. Berric was an exception but, over time, he became a strain with his constant demand to tell stories of mischief and sex.

Amarille was the first person I felt I could talk to without feeling drained afterwards, where I could actually find myself wishing a conversation would draw out longer.

After walking and remaining as quiet as possible to the chatty siblings and newly quiet prince, we make it back to the farm. The older man waits patiently outside in front of the barns. We come upon him as he's strapping a saddle to an all-black horse.

"Father!"

The two missing family members run over and nearly topple the man in a hug. He laughs with an ear-to-ear smile as he tries to wrap his frail arms around his two children who are much bigger than him. He continues to smile as he looks over at me, noticing my leg covered in blood.

"Are you okay, Mister?" he asks.

"Been through worse, nothing nearly as painful as what would have happened to your children."

"The guards stole them in the end?"

"Weren't guards. Instead, thugs and thieves with armour too big for their own ambitions."

He looks over at his children and wipes some of his tears with his wrist.

"Get back inside, you two. Food is waiting," he says.

The children anxiously nod their heads and then turn to me and hug me tightly. I don't bother attempting to refuse their offer but do not wrap my arms around them either, keeping one at my side and the other resting on the hilt of my blade.

"Thank you again!" Janun says before walking with Lyra into the main home, out of sight.

The older man puts a hand to his chest, smiling, and sits down onto a hay bale.

"Words cannot describe the service you have done for me, but I hope this is a start."

He points up towards the black horse with a fresh black saddle matching its fur and a few saddlebags around its back. Upon closer inspection, I notice that the horse is blind, two glazed balls for eyes.

"She's a blind horse?" Eli speaks up, reaching over and petting her fur.

"Aye, but the fastest." He sits up and pets her snout. "She is called Callie."

"She will do fine," I say. "We should get a move on to Olgierdum's first town before nightfall hits us."

"If there is anything else I can do, let me know. You two will always be welcome here…"

"Vesten," I say. "This here is Eli."

"Elliot, is fine."

I hop on the horse and help Eli up with one hand.

"Can I offer you two up some coin?" He struggles to reach into a pocket to hustle up a few gold pieces.

"Not needed, spend it on your family," I say.

I grab a hold of the reins before looking down at the older man again. "Look, if any of these people ever come back or pose a threat, although I doubt they will, send a raven for me, set for Aestas Isle. I will assure no one poses a threat to you and your family."

I click my tongue and let the horse know it's time to move. Going straight into a gallop, I hold the reins in one hand and keep one hand always over the hilt of my sword. Eli holds himself onto the sides of my jacket in order to not fall off on the often bumpy terrain. North from here, I know we'll find the first main town in Olgierdum, a place I visited once before called Olgierd's Rum.

I never actually knew if Olgierdum was named after someone or if Olgierd's Rum was a simple play on words of the province. It's a province filled with deep history, with most of the wars being in the dead centre of the two opposing sides. However, the first major town you come across is a play on the province's name.

"We should find a town and inn very soon, boy," I say to the back of the horse, trying to make my voice louder than the wind.

"Will there still be wanted posters if we plan on staying in another inn?"

"Not likely in the centre of Olgierdum. Most of the province isn't really in either kingdom's control enough for wanted posters to make their way into the mainstream. Anyone that knows about us will have had to come from either kingdom first." I move some of my hair from my face. "After this inn, however, we are pretty much on our own if we were not already before."

The horse ride is silent except for the clomping of hooves and wind whistling through our eyes until, off in the distance, I see the town. Absurdly small with no tall buildings, even from a distance, it seems to be a mini version of something much bigger you'd find in the kingdoms where all expenses can be spared.

Just like when I first visited, there are no town homes. I suppose this town has to primarily rely on farmers and people coming from either kingdom with no place to stay for the night, so they end up settling in the town.

There are a few shops around the main inn in the centre but not many. It wouldn't even surprise me if all of the shopkeepers knew each other by name. There's a strange mix of sand and grass. This far north, it's beginning to look more like a rotted grassland. The heat is still unbearable, but it's nothing compared to the heat of Summerwind.

Verenden is known for its intense change in weather, one kingdom covered in sand while the other is covered in snow. They're not even that far off from each other, a few days to a few weeks maybe. Soon we'll be too cold just as we are getting used to being too hot.

I bring Callie up to the inn, where only one other horse is attached to the post, meaning that this town is essentially dead this time of year. I came here when I was younger and more naïve, lucky enough to be in a situation where the crew I was with made anything dull into something interesting.

I hop off the horse and tie her onto the post so she does not go anywhere. Eli nearly falls off, landing on one foot and tilting himself to not trip while eventually falling close behind me.

We walk into the Inn, easily the smallest one we've been in so far. There seems to be a couple of rooms on both my left and my right with tables scattered throughout. I walk over and take a seat at one of the tables. Eli pulls a chair out and joins me. A barmaid sits in the corner reading, making eye contact for a brief moment before going back to her book.

Everything feels…still. There are a few people scattered at some other tables drinking without making too much of a fuss. Every word that comes out of anyone's mouth seems to be amplified by the lack of any sort of ambience. It's just utter quiet.

"Thank you," Eli says, breaking the silence.

"For what?" I slide the chair over closer to him so as to not risk anyone hearing our whispers.

"Not accepting the money. It wouldn't have been fair, accepting money and a horse when he was already housing two wanted men."

"He did not know we were wanted, what do you mean?" I tilt my head.

"I saw our wanted posters in the barn underneath some hay." We both laugh.

"Well…I guess he was smart betting on the two of us."

The barmaid finally puts down her book and walks up to serve us. Her black hair runs down to her dark-skinned shoulders.

"Can I get you two anything?" Her voice is stern and somewhat reminds me of my wife. One that demands respect. One I very much enjoy.

"One ale for me," I say.

"One for me, as well," Eli chimes in, smiling.

"I think not," I say. I watch the now smiling woman leave our table and I lean over to Eli. "I cannot have a hungover prince on the road."

"I wouldn't get—"

"Don't argue it, please." I rub my temples. "Wait, you found our wanted poster? What else did you snoop around at?"

"Nothing," he says confidently.

"Good."

"It's just—"

I sigh. "Oh gods."

"Who is the girl in your journal? The drawings, I mean?" I can feel him biting his tongue, not knowing if what he said would in any way get me angry.

I guess it would be foolish if I were to yell at him anymore, especially with something I am not going through great lengths to hide.

"My wife…Amarille," I decide to admit.

"Do you miss her?" He seems to be genuinely curious.

"Everyday."

The woman walks over and places the orange tinted ale in front of me in a wooden tankard. She smiles at Eli before walking away behind me towards the bar. I notice Eli follows her movements with his eyes.

"What is it like?" He inches closer to me, now essentially causing his chair to be connected to mine.

"What's what like? Marriage?"

"No, I mean like...you know" He motions to his chest and emphasizes it with his hands.

"You know if you wanna grow older, you gotta learn how to respect people," I say.

"Oh, yeah, of course!" He tries very hard while pretending I don't subtly notice him looking at the woman behind me.

"Boy, don't get me wrong. Both genders look at as many...'biological advantages' as much as one another but...that just isn't love."

"So what is love?"

"That's a loaded question, boy. The truth is, everyone you ask that question will give you some big speech about connection or something, but the best way to describe it is...you'll know it when it happens."

He laughs loudly, something I haven't actually heard before. "Your big advice...is you'll know it when it happens?"

"Well, yeah." I pound back the ale. "What would your father do?" I lean in to whisper. "What's the almighty king have to say about the matter?"

Suddenly Eli's smile disappears, and instead he looks saddened and removes his gaze from the girl and aims it towards the splintered, wooden table.

"Sometimes he would go into the city and spend the night in a brothel. Mother would pretend that she did not know about it but..."

"She did."

"Everyone did, Vesten." He coughs. "Some nights, in his drunken slurred state, he would come into my room still half-naked and reeking of the most foul alcohol you could ever smell. He would basically throw a young woman from the city into my room and pay her to attempt to sleep with me."

"Fucking hells, I am sorry, Boy," I say, moving some of the ale over to him to sip on. "So he would force you to sleep with women from the city?"

"He would try...I could never you know...commit."

"Is that why you want to know about spending a night with a

woman? In hopes maybe it can make it easier for the next time the time comes?"

He takes a small sip of the alcohol and looks back up at me.

"Yeah," he says.

The bartender and inn owner woman comes back over and notices him drinking out of my cup. Filling it up and then walking back to her table, she brings over a second cup and pours another into it. I suppose from her angle it looks like an intense father-son conversation. "You know, Eli, I only ever slept with one woman."

"Fuck off," he snarls.

"No, I am serious. Amarille, the woman in my journal. The only girl I ever slept with is also the only girl I ever married."

"Wait." He finally has a grin on his face once more. "A mercenary that has only slept with one person? Seems kind of unheard of."

"Well that's because you don't know what it was like." I take a sip of the ale from my own cup. "I grew up with her, and she was always the only thing that ever made me truly happy. I used to fall asleep in a few seconds knowing the next morning I could sneak onto her property just to have another conversation, let alone glance at her."

"Did she feel the same way?"

"Gods no. In fact, she hated me." I laugh. "She didn't want to jeopardize whatever we had built as friends, and neither did I."

"So wait...how did you two end up together?"

"She told me that one day she and I were out hunting, and the truth is, I don't remember the day as clearly as her, anyway, while out hunting we stopped at this waterfall near her home in Summerwind. Instead of just walking by it like normal, she walks up to me and says she wants to try something. She just grabs me by my face and kisses me once. To this day, I still remember kissing her at that waterfall."

"And then I am guessing you two had sex, right?"

"First of all...mind your tongue. Second of all...not even close. It wasn't about the sex, boy, it was simply about affection. The first time I ever saw her naked was after we had both ran from her father's hound into a sauna, and she asked me to draw her, and even still...I remember her eyes more than her body."

"You know, Vesten, that sounds rather sweet coming from you."

"I imagine anything sounds sweet when not coming from your father."

"You know what the worst part of it is?" Eli laughs to himself, the alcohol no doubt affecting him. "I don't even really know much about my father. Sometimes the most I would ever see him would be when he tossed some poor girl into my room."

"My dads were similar…not in the same light as yours but close in a way. One of my dads taught me how to fight, how to respect people of any race or gender. All while my other dad was far away in a place called Eaforith teaching kids with quirks."

Eli reaches over and grabs my shoulder. "It's not like he wasn't there, he just…"

"Wasn't there." I stare down at my alcohol. "Well, I can drink to that." I finish my drink and stand up to go pay for a room. "Goodnight, Boy."

"Wait! Can you at least finish the sauna story?" He giggles.

"Ask about my naked wife again and I will—"

"Stab me with your sword?" He giggles.

I put one finger on my nose and then point it to him. "Exactly, Eli."

11

DEATHS PORT

I wake Eli up, and he gets up and gets ready in a flash. Gathering everything with record speed, we both head down the stairs. We're about to walk out of the door when I stop and turn back around.

"What are you doing?" Eli asks, walking behind me now.

"Just gotta do something real quick." I walk up to the inn owner who seems not to have many customers at this hour. "Do you take letters here?"

"Aye of course, so long as you have the paper."

"I do, thank you."

I pull out the small notebook from my coin purse latched around my side. Taking out the small quill, I dip it into the ink. Opening the notebook to a random blank page, I begin to write.

Dearest Amarille,
I have a lot of explaining to do and not a lot of paper. I have to bring a small boy named Eli back to his home. In return he will make it worth our while.
I am sorry.

I miss and love you and hope to be home soon

> Everything we do…well you know.
> -Vesten

I flip the letter over and write our home's raven nest on the paper. Some of the ink is bleeding into the paper, but nevertheless I hand it over to her. She takes it and nods, tucking it underneath the table.

"You didn't leave any information to get a letter sent back to you?" The inn owner tilts her head.

"Travelling quite a bit, would only cause confusion for the birds. Thank you again."

I waste no time before looking down at Eli and motioning my head up towards the door so he knows we can officially leave here. It looks as if he wants to speak up and ask about the letter but he stops, I suppose knowing it's beyond whatever you could call our friendship level.

Callie is nicely waiting outside for us, her fur freshly brushed, creating beautiful black streaks, her mouth full of food. She looks as happy and healthy as ever, which makes me feel a bit more at ease over the lack of plentiful coins.

I double check that the camping supplies are still strapped in tight. Two typical black wool bedrolls and some sticks with flint tucked into it. I know we won't be able to find an Inn by the end of the night with the distance we need to trek. We'll have to camp out over night for the first time in what feels like years.

I hop on the horse and help Eli onto the back, then tuck my legs in tightly so the horse begins her gallop. Back on the road again, it seems.

Death's Port, aptly named due to the fact that most who wash up on these shores are dead. There are no taverns around here out of respect. Instead, it is as barren and blunt as the legends surrounding it. It technically is not even legal in any empires to park your boat here for fear of damaging the spirits' wills or something along those lines.

I, like most people, don't believe the legends to an extent…but I am not going to be the poor soul that awakens any demons when I have a pregnant wife at home.

We trek on for a little bit, keeping the horse in a slight trot to utilize its stamina as best we can. No matter what, we won't be able to get to Remorse in Slimhixe until we traverse Death's Port and Families' Echoes. Should be a dull affair compared to the usual thing we've been getting used to. Fighting and death wherever we go from either my side of the empire or from Eli's, trying to 'save' their prince.

I feel a slight bit of snow touch the tip of my nose. I look up towards the sky at the insane difference between where we trot now compared to where we were a few hours ago. The blistering heat has been replaced by a slight chill in the air and your lungs as you breathe. Slimhixe is essentially a frozen wasteland compared to the south, and now we are essentially dead in the centre of both.

I don't hate the weather. Part of me wishes the Aestas Isle would be more like this. A climate where it's never blistering you in sweat or leaving your bones chilled like a metal sword left out overnight in the snowbank.

"So, Eli," I say to break the silence as we trot along. "Anything I should know about Slimhixe before we arrive there eventually?"

"Do you know about the Frozen Horses?" he asks.

"You guys keep frozen horses out? For what reasons?"

"No, not like that. The Frozen Horses are the royal guards of the king. Big brutes of men and women who carry giant hammers and wear long fur coats around their armour. Ought to weigh a few hundred pounds all together, but they are savage, that's for sure."

"Their helmets resemble a horse?"

"Yeah, and their armour is that of a mountain lion. I doubt even your fancy sword could pierce through it."

"I remember them." I stare down at the reins in between my hands. "The leader of each barrack for a town has gold across their armour."

"Yeah! Mother would always tell me that I would end up growing up to become one."

"Your mother…was she kind to you or was she like your father?" I decide to switch gears from the talk of advanced guards that only bring up bad memories.

"You know it's funny, Vesten…everyone in Slimhixe has these ideals and ways about thinking. As if everyone is better than one another, and no one is superior to their own wit….not my mother, however. She just seemed like a normal girl caught up in a war my father started."

"If she was normal, why marry a king?" I ask.

"She used to tell me about how when they first met she was the only woman for him. Nothing else in the world mattered except their love...then with him becoming king, the stress, the drink, and the whores that can plunder away sorrows quicker than talking out your problems...it changed the man."

"I am sorry for her," I say. "Can't imagine anyone ever imagines they are going to end up with a king. Let alone one that is so against the times."

"How is he against the times?" Eli now sounds offended.

"You know, Eli...I had a son once named Erron." I stop the horse for a second and take a deep breath. "He had his mother's eyes more than my own, but he had our hair. Everything in him was a perfect blend of my wife and me. There were some parts of him you could predict before he was born. That he would end up having our combined hair color and one of our eyes...but we couldn't predict the quirk."

"He had a quirk?"

"The fire one, to be specific. Not even the dastardly blood one everyone always preaches on about. He was no more than ten. My wife, Amara, would always tell me not to worry and that it would be fine. *Surely* the empire we had devoted our lives to would never harm him."

"You still were with my empire at this time, right?" he asks.

"Yes." I cough slightly, trying to be rid of the tears forming in my eyes. "Then one day, while I was out on the water, and Amara was north of Aestas buying stock, we came back to find him gone. Rushing to Slimhixe, we found him tied to a stake put in the ground by a set of guards wearing metal masks that looked like horses, one of them bearing a golden stripe along his armour. People gathered from all around and came to watch a ten-year-old boy die at the stake because he was born different."

"Vesten, I—"

"It's true, what they say. All what they say about having a child is true. That you never truly believed you could love something more than yourself or your significant other until they came around. He was every perfect part of us, he did not have the gray background like I or the troubled childhood of Amarille. He was pure, but because he awoke one night with a small flicker of a flame at his fingertip, he was ignited into ash."

"I—I—am so sorry." Eli sniffles.

"It wasn't you. It was your father…I still remember it all, Eli. The boat ride over to Slimhixe, the smoke, the screaming, the look in his eyes when he saw his two parents clawing forward trying to reach out for him."

"Why would my father do this?"

"In his eyes, people with quirks should be feared, thrown away like a commonplace item that no longer serves a use."

"When my father is dead, though…I can change that rule, right?" He wipes his tears with his sleeve.

"I hope you can be a better man than your father…for me, though,

it doesn't matter if you change the laws for future children. I still lost my boy to the stake, and Slimhixe will forever hold his life in their hands. Your father could not offer me a price or law to forgive the screams."

Eli once again wipes some of the tears from his face. He stares down as if embarrassed by the things his father has done. It's not surprising he didn't know about the burnings, or even if he had, maybe his father told him that it was only done to criminals. A young child burning could quickly become a murderer if the words left the ever-so-graceful king's mouth. "A son should not be held for the treasons of his father."

The rest of the horse ride is quiet. As we finally reach Death's Port, I decide we should rest up for the night. I rest Callie at a smaller pine tree. I take a close look at the environment around us. It's like most places north of a forest, but the trees are not very high. The snow, although falling, doesn't leave much of a blanket around our feet, and we can still see the frosty grass underneath our boots where we step. Just past the forest are mountains and open fields as far as the eye can see.

We're technically not even that close to Death's Port as that would require us to go straight to the water, which would end up causing us to travel for a longer period of time. Nevertheless, I feel like even this close to it should be enough to keep any common thug away from our coin purse. Just close enough to Slimhixe and Families' Echoes so we are just far enough away that a typical merchant won't run into us.

I hop off the horse and pull out the camping supplies, flinging out both wool bedrolls. I place the flammable sticks on the ground. Grabbing some nearby snowy rocks from underneath trees, I place a small circle around the makeshift bonfire.

I take the flint and slide my sword to it. I watch the sparks fly off until hitting the highly flammable stick and igniting it almost instantly in a large burst. The orange hue hits my face with bright warmth as I grab some more sticks lying around and throw them into the flames.

"Get some rest, Eli," I say. "Another day of travel ahead of us tomorrow."

"Okay," he whispers solemnly, no doubt still processing the story I told him on the ride here.

I assure the fire is good and able to last us a long while before tucking myself underneath the wool sheet of my bedroll and placing my head against the frozen, small pillow sewed into the fabric at the top. Staring up at the trees, I see only small bits of snow fall and hit my face. I close my eyes.

"Your sword is named after your son, isn't it?" Eli breaks the silence.

I sniffle slightly, still not fully over the conversation from earlier. "Yes...now get some sleep."

***

"You have another new scar?" I hear the sweet and newly concerned voice of my wife behind me as the hot water pours over my naked body.

I turn, wiping my hair and the water from my eyes to take a look at her displeased in her robes.

"Lovely to see you too, darling."

"What's the new scar from? The one slashed right on the bottom of your back." She crosses her arms.

"I have...always had that one," I say, trying to be convincing but knowing she can probably see right through me.

"No." She walks closer to the open shower in the corner of our room and turns me around forcefully. "You have plenty of scars but this one is new."

She presses her fingers into the freshly stitched wound, and I let out a small grunt of pain.

"It's simple, I got it from a bear."

"There are not any bears on Aestas...unless all of a sudden there are, and they wield swords?"

I turn back to face her. "What? Did you kill them all?"

"Actually, *Froh'v*, I read about it." She leans in and kisses me gently.

"It was from no one, just a spy from Summerwind while I was out and about."

"Is the spy still with us?" She plays with the top of my wet hair. Noticing my lack of a response is the answer. "Good."

"What is new—"

"So, Vest...I have been thinking." She seems rather nervous.

"Thinking about what?" I wash the last bits of soap from my body and walk out of the shower onto the wooden floor and over towards our clothing cupboard.

"A child," she says.

I stop looking for anything to cover myself and instead turn to face her.

"Is now the best time to discuss this?" I say, looking down at my body and then back up at her.

"We have discussed this before...and I quite enjoy the view."

I laugh. "What is left to discuss?"

"Just think, *Froh'v*...a child could be our new start." She walks up to me and places a hand on the v line of my stomach. "Away from the lives our weapons had taken us and towards a family. You built the home we stand in, and I am sure we can find other careers that do not involve as much bloodshed."

She takes a step backwards, gently sliding her fingers over my skin until she's out of grasp. She undoes a button on the top of her robe, and then another, slowly, until it falls to the floor and gets kicked away by her feet. Now the two of us are naked in the candlelit room as the snow trickles down outside.

I come closer to her, wrapping my arms around her waist and bringing her in close for a kiss.

"We are young," I say. "Only twenty-four years of age. Are you sure this would be the right decision?"

"In my mind…yes." She bites the lower part of my lip. "But do not answer for the sole reason that I expose myself to you. I will continue to do so until we die, and you and I are old and not as pleasurable to stare at."

"I wouldn't have it any other way." I smile, moving my hands from her waist down.

"I am serious *F'rohv*! Make this decision with your heart and not your…" She takes a step back and stares below my waist. "Sword."

"I do want a child." I laugh. "Only with you, only if you are certain, and only if you are sure the time is right."

"Well, Vest." She snickers, reminding me of how she used to when we were kids, and I realized it was quickly becoming a favorite feature of hers to me. "I suppose we should get a head start right now then." She pulls me onto the bed.

12

ERRONS SPIRE

Where am I? I hear the constant stream of people talking amongst themselves, deafening any train of thought that attempts to start. I try and push my way through the shadowy figures that are close enough for me to rub elbows with them.

I push, and I shove, trying to get through them as their words become louder and louder, eventually sounding as if each individual whisper is a scream banging in my ears. I clutch my hands together and continue to move forward through the crowd. I feel myself trip and fall to the ground.

Slamming my body into the pavement, I look around at everyone surrounding me, only they're not people, just shapeless faces and slim, tall bodies that remind me of trees. Their piercing black bodies and faces lack human emotion continue to whisper in my ears. I feel myself try and get on my feet. After a few attempts, I manage to stand up and reach over to draw *Erron* from my side.

I grasp nothing except my own palm as I look over and realize I do not have a blade to fight these monstrosities, only fists and typical brown leather armour.

Their whispers still pierce my ear drums to the point of blood falling and dripping onto the concrete underneath me. The loud sounds are now deafening. It feels like my hearing has ceased to function, replaced by an ongoing searing pain at a mere whisper.

Red rain once again pours over everything.

I clasp my hands to my ears and take a few deep breaths. I run towards the front of the group of people, somewhere away that I can finally escape the lanky, gaze-less abominations that refuse to do anything other than whisper. Finally, I reach the end of these things.

I fall onto my knees, my ears spewing blood like a waterfall that I cannot contain with my palms. Stopping with the whispers, I stare down at the concrete covered in the red thick blood. My hearing only comes back to me in small increments with slight yelling and...crackles of a fire?

I look up to see Erron, his hands bound behind him on the stake. I attempt to stand up before I feel the shadowy figures pull me back to look up towards the red raining sky. A slight tinge of black smoke meets it in the corner of my vision from Erron's spire. I try to speak but nothing comes out, or at least nothing I can hear. I am trampled and covered by the shadowy figures as I attempt to escape. I kick, shove, and scream as much as I can, but eventually my vision is covered by the black of the dark figures and red of the ever-pouring rain. Finally, everything is black.

"If it's a girl," I hear Amara say, though I see nothing but black. "If it's a girl...Ellia. If it's a boy...**Erron**."

The darkness splits away with a flash, causing my retinas to feel a burn. I rub them to try and see the spire in which my son is confined. Only his body is covered in ash and tar with some skin falling away from his legs and feet with his burned clothes. He falls into my arms, and I lean him towards the ground as he groans in pain and lets out a few squeals.

I bring his head down onto my lap, his hand clutching mine as my other wraps around his cheek. Staring into his blood shot eyes, my tears fall onto his charred skin.

"Don't let me die, Dad, please. I am not ready to die," he cries out to me.

"I will never let you die. I got you Erron."

"It's dark, everything is dark. Why is everything dark?"

His body goes limp. It feels like he's just doubled his weight as the last breath escapes with a slight squeal that sounds more painful to me than the shadows that seem to have vanished.

"I got you Erron," I cry over him. "I got you, Little Fox, do not worry."

* * *

I awake on the dirt floor, this time the cold sweat not my main focus as I feel a sharp tip pierce my gambeson and stare up at an unfamiliar face. It's a tall, rugged man with stubble along his face and a few scars underneath his cheeks behind his smile.

I attempt to turn to the side to see if Eli is still lying beside me but instead feel his boot press down on my chest while he aims his longsword towards my neck with a shorter sword in his other hand tucked away at his hip. No fresh blood on the steel means that he has not recently used it to kill Eli, so I know I can rest easy for the moment and hope Eli at least tried to make a run for it.

"How can I be of assistance?" I ask with the sweat still dripping along my forehead from my new nightmare.

"Was deep in town for a little." The rasp in his voice sounds more rustic than an anchor that hasn't been raised in years. "Saw a poster and decided to track you…actually expected you two to present more of a challenge. Not from around here are you? Otherwise, you would have known that hooves don't disappear as much in the south as they would up north."

"You must have the wrong guy, friend," I try to reason but feel him press harder with his boot into the centre of my chest.

"Don't believe I do," he says with a smirk. "Don't worry, I will make sure the boy doesn't feel much."

"If you so much as look at him, I will—"

"What? Use the sword I kicked over there?" He tilts his head up towards my right, and I look over to see the open grass. There is no sword there. "What the—"

"Ahh!" I hear Eli scream from behind him as he slashes once at the man's leg, causing him to fall. Eli looks scared and is gritting his teeth.

He takes a swipe with my sword, slashing away at the man, who falls onto his side. Eli rushes him, plunging it farther and farther into his face as it concaves itself into a bloody pool.

"Eli!" I yell, trying to remove him as he continues to slash faster and faster. He throws the sword away just as it gets bright orange and watches the lightning crack as it hits the grass and slides in with its bloody, sharp blade.

Eli stares down at the guy and then back up at me, tears falling from his face before he reaches out and lunges at me for a hug. I wrap my arms around him and bring his face deep into my shoulder as he sobs.

"I didn't—I never—I—" He sobs into me. I run my hands through the back of his hair, trying to show as much affection as I can.

"Look at me!" I move him away as he keeps his eyes closed and continues to cry while I brush his tears away with my thumb. "I got you Elliot, I got you…it's okay."

* * *

THE NIGHT still feels young as Eli tries his best to sleep. I keep watch until the orbs begin to shine light once more. I pay extra close attention to the snow to make sure our tracks are covered so no one else can follow us so easily.

Was I that dumb? Did I *seriously* not think to cover my tracks? Elliot and I could be standing on Death's Port staring out at the sea, and they still would have been able to find us due to my carelessness.

Elliot finally stops crying after a while, with just the occasional slight sob or whimper as he tries to sleep but can't. I look over at him and notice he still has had no luck, his back turned away from me as every few seconds he sniffles and moves his arm to wipe a tear.

I walk over the bandit's body that I moved a few metres away from myself and the tent. The blood trail leads me to his mutilated corpse, face still seeming to ooze some blood if even remotely touched. I search around his body and find his short sword, lifting it up and feeling it.

It's a simple small blade, no crossguard, engraving, or proper weight, but small and light enough that it should do the trick.

I walk over to Elliot as he attempts to sleep and stab the blade into the ground behind his back. He jumps and turns back to me, standing up and wiping his tears once more.

"What the fuck is this? Are you trying to make me remember what the fuck just happened?"

"No." I remain cold. "You won't be able to forget...but you will be able to learn. Now pick up the sword."

"What?"

"Pick it up," I tell him, drawing my sword. I notice the white blade matches the falling snowflakes. "And slash."

I spread my feet apart and bend my legs slightly to brace myself, clutching the blade in two hands and watching him lift the sword, still crying slightly. He walks over to me and slashes lightly at my blade, barely knocking it from its default pointed position.

"Why are we doing this, Vesten?"

"Bend your knees. You are training, not dancing. Hold your sword like I am."

I hold my hands toward him, watching him take a second and wipe his tears on his sleeve for the last time before brushing his short black hair with his fingers and grasping the blade.

"Is this okay?"

"Perfect, now strike at me, Elliot, and put your weight behind it!"

He slashes once more at my blade, this time causing me to move slightly off balance. "Again!"

He continues to slash away as I walk backwards.

"This is pointless," he tries to chime in, but I continue to move back with the clanks of his sword.

"Follow my feet, never get caught off guard. Your position is just as important as your skills with a blade...now block!"

I swing my sword with one hand as his survival instinct kicks in, and with both hands he blocks the blade. "Brilliant, Elliot! Guide my blade if you are not physically stronger!"

I continue slashing more and more, now with his new blade getting closer to becoming an extension of himself. He is able to redirect my heavier attacks. Even redirecting one into the snow. The orange glow of my blade starts to form as I continue to move forward at him, slashing.

I back away from him and jam the sword into the snow, the sparks and thunder emitting directly in front of it. I bring myself back up with the white blade, but he seems to have dropped his arms, blade now dangling.

"I am weak, Vesten. I could barely hold down a whimper let alone my emotions from killing the man."

"Do you believe tears are a sign of weakness? Maybe in the eyes of a lesser man like the king, but he does not fight." I walk over to him and lean, pressing my hand into his shoulder. "I could barely stand my first kill either. Humanity is not and will never be a weakness. Now lift your sword and practice your spin!" Once again, he regains himself.

The cold snow falls over both of us and the sun rises over the mountains, hitting us gently with its orange light. He clutches his blade and practices his spin, clearly not spotting his spin as he falls quite quickly.

"I—um, don't know how to spin well." He finally smiles and laughs to himself. His red, tear-filled eyes are aglow in the new light pressing against his face.

"So we will practice." I laugh. "Can't have a companion on a journey who does not know how to spin."

He walks over and grabs the short sword he is holding by the blade, tilting the hilt towards me to grab it.

"Here," he says, smiling up at me.

"No…keep it. You really saved me back there, and you are right. You do deserve a sword at least."

"Really?"

"Aye, that being said, you will need to do some more training, but we will find time before slumber or in the mornings. I bet when we get back to Slimhixe, you'll be rather decent."

I turn and am about to walk past him when he reaches an arm out and puts it on my arm.

"Vesten…thank you. For everything, I cannot say what my fate would have become without you."

"Well, Elliot, I guess we always gotta find purpose in life, and it took me a few nightmares to realize that maybe I've been too hard on you."

"Really? Does this mean you will start treating me better?"

"Don't push your luck." I laugh with him and pat him on the shoulder as I walk towards the horses. "In my family, our motto is, 'A fox in the spring travels without a choice.'"

"What does that mean?" He takes both his hands and rubs his eyes, finally done with tears for the night…or I guess morning now.

"In Klikia where I was born, every spring, most animals would hibernate. Foxes, wolves, and even bears, all because Verenden is home to many dangerous creatures that come out only during the spring. So basically, the saying is trying to mean that no matter what, we must always find a way to survive."

"Is that why people call you Fox?"

I take a minute and breathe. The winter air chills my lungs slightly with the large inhale but reminds me of home. "Yeah…yeah it is, Elliot."

13

FAMILIES ECHOES & ALL IT MEANS

"Essentially," I say, laughing with Elliot, "in order to fully…satisfy your partner, it is all about communication."

"So, like, asking about what they like?"

"Exactly that, then you will be a better husband and lover to whomever you choose to commit to."

"Sounds easy enough," he laughs.

"You know, Elliot?" I place a hand over his shoulder as we walk. "I think she will really like you."

"Really?"

"Oh, for sure. My wife has a thing for people who speak their mind." I laugh with him.

"I sure hope she is much nicer than you upon first meeting," he says.

"Well, it depends…"

"On?"

"If you are a bear or something, then she will put an arrow between your eyes."

We both continue our way through Olgierdum. Callie keeps a pace that I know will get us straight to Slimhixe so long as we do not get into any more trouble from unwanted guests that appear in the night.

After a few hours of riding and sharing stories about our upbringing, we are now approaching Families' Echoes.

I halt the horse. Elliot tries to peek past me at the next stop on the road. I hop off the horse and wrap the reins around my left hand. I help Elliot off the horse, and we get a move on. Off in the distance, I see large mounds in the ground, ash along with countless bodies: metal armour plates filled with skeletons and decomposing corpses; limbs torn off and thrown away from their host body; weapons scattered all over the muddy hills, filling with gentle snow, and even some siege weapons fallen over and now seemingly mixing into the ground.

"Wait a minute." Eli runs over to a few of the corpses as we approach. Flipping over a few metal chest plates, he reveals the Slimhixe insignia etched now in ash and dried blood. "These are mainly Slimhixe bodies?"

"Aye, this is where the battle of Families' Echoes took place. The forefront of both empires clashing against each other."

Elliot continues to flip over more bodies, uncover more banners, and check the helmets of the group of corpses. Again, only the Slimhixe insignia is found. Eventually he comes across one Summerwind loyal bound body compared to the five more of Slimhixe.

"This isn't a battlefield…it is essentially a graveyard for my people!"

"Your father did not tell you about this battle, did he?"

Elliot shakes his head, the look of anger and disgust overwhelming him.

"This is Slimhixe's greatest defeat to date, the battle that would not only define Summerwind as a contender for power in Verenden but where everything would change."

"But why? How did Slimhixe lose?" He almost spits at the thought of his all-glorious hometown falling in battle.

I reach an arm out and stop him from searching, pulling him gently towards one of the many large mounds in the ground. Staring into it, I notice the ash and snow, weapons tinged in black soot and armour pieces charred.

"What do you think caused this?" I ask.

"Siege weapons?" He looks over at me.

"Wrong." I take a deep breath. "Mages."

"But...how did mages do this? They are outlawed!" He stares back at the mound, now noticing the hundreds that fill the distance past the reaches of our vision.

"No one thought Summerwind would be a contender for the throne. Slimhixe brought their armies and cavalry out to this field to meet them in head-to-head combat close to the border of Slimhixe. In fact, your empire was winning most of the battle until Summerwind revealed the one thing that Slimhixe would never in a million years think to use."

"Mages," Elliot whispers with some of his breath leaving a sort of smoke in front of his lips with the cold.

"In Slimhixe they banned mages for their destructive capabilities. In Summerwind *they invited it.*"

I grab Eli and assure he gets a move on to keep on pace. The entire time he looks around at the bodies and attempts to maintain a strong composure at the eerie atmosphere.

"How come Summerwind didn't win? How come I am still breathing along with my father?"

"By the time the mages were introduced, the numbers of Summerwind's non-magic forces, they were few to none...they did not have the resources to claim a throne, only destroy one."

"So they just gave up? And after all that, my father didn't once think about investing the help of mages?" Elliot once again sounds angry.

"Why would he? Summerwind's entire empire is born on the belief quirk users are evil. It would go against what he had tried to preach to your people for thousands of years."

Elliot stops walking for a moment, turning towards me.

"Your son had a quirk, and he died in my empire. That is why you switched to Summerwind allegiance right?"

"Aye," I say coldly to him. "Upon a pyre, he was burnt in front of your town because he was born with something he could not control."

"And now my empire? Is what? Just waiting for the end?" Elliot goes back to walking.

"Essentially, yes, your father will die with his so-called ambition.

However, nothing compared to the countless lives he has already taken."

"Stop, you two!" I hear a female voice call out from behind us. Three bandits ride up on horses. All hop off in front and stare at us.

Elliot goes to draw his sword and I immediately bring my hand down and keep him from removing his blade from the sheathe.

"Sheathe your sword!" I lean down and say to him.

"Why? Aren't they about—" He looks over at the bandits, who, although carrying weapons, have not drawn and instead walk holding their horses much like us.

"People believe Families' Echoes is cursed, that all the gods would smite someone who dares attempt to draw blood on these grounds."

"We are here for the bounty, old man." The female leader snarls at me.

"Well, you have found us, although you do understand the situation the gods have put us in?" I motion towards the corpses and battlefield.

"Aye, we won't make any of you bleed until we are off this cursed place. I imagine you dare not attempt the same." The female one snarls.

"Aye," I reply. "I wouldn't like to test my fight anymore than I already have...I do suppose we should get a move on."

I turn around with Elliot and pull the reins forward. We make our way through the battlefield. The three bandits pull their horses to the side and eyeball us. One on my left and two on my right, closer to where Elliot stands around me. I hear nothing but the sounds of winter snow falling and the pressed, compact crunch our boots leave in the little amount of snow. Occasionally, someone kicks or trips by accident on a helmet or sword scattered around, but nevertheless we all continue walking as if we are normal travel companions.

"How much longer do we need to walk for?" one of the male bandits asks.

"Shut up, Twig!" the female leader shouts before looking at Elliot and me.

"So," I say, deciding I might as well try and reason with them.

"How much exactly are they paying you for the life of a poor father and son?"

"Don't play games with us," the other male one to my left says.

"We know the boy is the prince."

Fuck.

We all walk side by side until, eventually, I see the end of Families' Echoes, the battlefield and scattered bodies replaced by an open field of snow. Except, there are already people there. Two guards stand in large armour, long war hammers at their sides. I'd recognize the armour anywhere, the Frozen Horses, Slimhixes's true military prowess.

"Halt," one of them yells through the long metal helmet resembling a horse's snout. "The boy comes with us, and you must face the judgement of the king!"

"Come quietly, or there will be force!" the female one to the guard's side chirps in.

"Hey! This lot of fucks is ours! We had 'em first!" The female one snarls at the guards as I walk a few feet closer to the guards standing about a metre away from them now.

The group of people disperse into a circle, two bandits on my right, one bandit on my left, and two frozen horse guards directly in front of me.

"Gentlemen and ladies, perhaps there can be a simple solution to our troubles?" I reach to my side and hold up my coin purse.

"Fuck off!" the male bandit yells. "Cross the barrier so we can kill you away from the gods' wrath, you coward!"

The two guards in front of me hold their hammers out in front of themselves. I place one hand over *Erron* and simply wait.

"Hand them over, old man!" the guard snarls.

"You are all wrong, though." I smirk. "For one, I am not that old. Rather young, I like to imagine, and second...the barrier line was back a few feet."

With a swift movement, I lift *Erron* from its sheath along my side and slash at the bandit on my left, who, without having any time to react, gets slashed directly in his chest and falls to the ground. Elliot seems to have caught on and has already slashed at the second bandit's knees with his short sword before slashing again and lodging his blade into his neck.

The female bandit lifts up her club impaled with nails that she wields like someone would a kitchen knife to fight off an intruder, hunched over, and feral. She is just about to dive for me when she is slammed in the back by the guards' two hammers.

The two guards both fling their weapons in unison behind their back so the blunt end is facing the snow. Elliot moves directly to my side and tries to mimic the way I hold my blade with both my hands, twisting his hands when I do and even copying my footwork like I told him to do. I move away from Elliot and swing my blade to my sides trying to build up the orange hue.

"Do not make us hurt you, little prince. Come with us or—"

"Ahhh!" Elliot screams as he runs towards the guard on the right, slashing away with his short sword and using his slightly small stature and small sword to his advantage as he cuts the male guard's shin with his blade.

The female guard notices him doing this and raises her arms above her head, about to bring the hammer down like a woodcutter would cut a log. I put my sword into one hand and brandish it, the orange hue finally reaching its peak as she slams down and looks over at me. A large bolt of lightning fires out and hits her helmet clean off while sending her back a few feet.

I walk over to Elliot and smile at him, patting the side of his arm with my hand.

"Nice job, kid," I say to him.

His hands shake, and he throws up onto the snow.

"Won't my father know we butchered these guards?" He looks up.

"What do you mean?" I point over towards the bandits. "This was clearly a fight we never took part in. A simple fight where no one won."

Elliot nods. I can see through him that he is trying his best to be tough but failing as his eyes give way to a few tears that melt the snow beneath him.

"This is all fucked, Vesten."

I walk over to him and bring him in for a hug. This time, he does not spend so much time crying as much as he does hugging back.

"Aye, it is fucked. But it's either them or us, and you gotta remember that. Prince or not, the poster says alive or dead."

"I hate it, all of this death over what? Money? Loyalty?"

"The truth is, Elliot, when all is said and done, all that remains from true morals while we are out here are the last of us. If we do not kill them, they will kill us. It is us against the world, against both empires until you are home, and even then, I do not know if I will get a pardon."

"I will make sure you do!"

"You will try, but from everything I hear about your father, it sounds like the king doesn't think forgiveness is a good political tactic."

"So why continue? Why keep me all the way from the south of Verenden to the north?"

"Let's get a move on, boy."

Long have their bodies roat.
A quicker death than a noose tied taught.
For the gaze of the gods you will meet.
That of echoes they will call, a repeated curse you must keep back.
Soldiers piled high, for what was between their ears and behind their eyes.
A mind lost and yours to follow, lay down your sword oh dear old fellow.

    -Orieon Virel, Shanties Of Verenden, Tome 2.

14

A SIMPLE TOWN CALLED REMORSE

Welcome to Remorse, east of Families' Echoes, and the last town before arriving directly at the heart of Slimhixe where the king sits upon his throne. There are all concrete buildings around the back of the town and a more modest front near the centre where we enter and mount our horse.

There is a diverse group of townspeople compared to the majority of Elves that you see when you head south. A few Dragonkin people walk around and purchase goods, even some goblins and orcs, although they seem to have been brought up here and are not from Veritas where most of their kinds tend to stay. A mother and her child walk down the street hand in hand as they eat some frozen sweet treat.

Also, of course, there are fire spires sprung up and covered in ash in case any Mages decide to expose themselves inside this town. Moving past it, you can even smell decomposed flesh and tar, but no one else that lives here seems to notice, all continuing to go on with their lives as if everything is normal.

The snow is finally falling at a rate I am accustomed to, firm blankets of white surrounding the concrete grounds and more falling from the sky as we put Callie in a stable to stay warm and fed.

"So this is Remorse." I look over at Elliot before handing the stable master a few gold pieces. "Not exactly a *good* sounding name."

"Well, I suppose the people who made it were cryptic." He quotes my words from before.

"Well played," I say with a laugh.

I take a look around and try to absorb the surroundings. Oddly enough, there aren't many of our wanted posters. I imagine they would probably think we are heading south as opposed to north due to the 'kidnapping' of a prince. An attempt for leverage in the war when in reality I am bringing him straight towards his insane father. Luckily for me, Elliot really hasn't been much of a face for Slimhixe. Everything he has done has been under the guise of his father, so he never needed to visit towns proclaiming his hierarchy.

I still have a few gold coins, and I know I'll be able to spend a bit on drinks tonight as a celebration for making it this far without either of us losing any limbs. I doubt Amarille will be able to believe the lengths to which I've gone for this boy. I imagine she will not be too pleased at first, scolding me and telling me I am the dumbest person she has ever met. It did feel good to stray away from ships and actually be able to talk to someone that isn't as bloodthirsty as Berric used to be and whom I can actually teach things.

It does feel odd, being this long away from my wife, not being able to see her after a long day of fighting people or doing insane things all for the benefit of our family. I miss being able to rant to her about my day, and now it seems I am left speaking with Elliot about my problems, even though I don't wholeheartedly mind the boy's company. It feels good protecting someone that truly is in need of help and not just looking for extra muscle to appear imposing.

Elliot and I walk around the town, nearly getting to the border of it where we can see the high walls before seeing an Inn/Tavern. 'Remorse-ful Drink' with a picture of a horse drinking straight from a tankard like it is a water bowl. I wonder if it is referencing the guards that come down here before taking their patrols east or if they just thought it would be a funny picture to etch into the board.

We walk in and are met with a few odd faces. An Orcish man and small goblin at his side with large ears discussing their lives back home in Veritas, the Goblin explaining a fire that had taken their home, and the orc understandably annoyed. A few elven people surround a large table in the centre discussing colleges east of here. Around them are a few different bartenders of many races, a few cleaning, and a few serving drinks.

I walk over to a table in the corner with two chairs and Elliot and I both sit down. Rubbing my eyes, I now realize how much of a toll this entire thing has taken on my body, nothing but fighting and lack of sleep meaning that, no matter what, I never get enough rest. Perhaps tonight will be different, and I will be able to visit a sauna to wipe away the mud from my hair.

"Can I get you two anything?" An Orcish man smiles at us with his two tusks pointing upwards from his lower jaw.

"One ale for me and one for the boy," I reply swiftly and put two gold pieces on the table.

Elliot looks over at me surprised, blinking a few times and trying to process what I just did.

"Did you just order me a drink? Whatever happened to no drunk company?"

"Well, the way I see it, we won't be in too much of a hassle from this point on, and I feel like you have deserved a small break."

"Thank you, Vesten." He smiles at me.

The Orcish man walks over and places two cups and a pitcher of alcohol on the table.

"The two gold pieces pay for way more than two cups." He smiles at us and walks back behind the counter where I notice a few other of the bartenders looking over at us.

I take the pitcher of blue alcohol and pour it into both of our cups. An absurd amount of alcohol that, on any other occasion, I would need an entire ship's crew in order to consume fully.

The Orcish man smiles and places down another pitcher just in front us and smiles at us some more. I think I may have underestimated the value of gold pieces this far north.

Elliot lifts his cup up in one hand in a toast to me.

"To nearly dying every fucking second." He smiles at me.

"Aye." I clank my cup against his, watching some contents spill out but drinking it regardless.

I watch Elliot take a large gulp as if it is water and immediately regret it as he gags slightly at the coarse alcohol that burns down his throat with an unpleasant feeling. However, he does continue to drink it a bit more moderately with me. Both of us drink a cup within a few minutes and pour ourselves more from the pitcher.

Within an hour, I feel my vision grow hazy, and Elliot begins to giggle like there is no tomorrow.

"So hold on." He snorts. "I am still so confused, you flipped over an entire fucking ship."

I cover my eyes from crying while laughing. "It is not that simple, I thought by spinning the wheel and forcing my crew to one side it would avoid spilling."

"So how did you slip—flip the ship?" He wipes a tear from his eyes.

"I made them move to the same side I was turning towards." I laugh hysterically with Elliot.

Pouring another cup of the alcohol, I drink while laughing into the tankard. A few more minutes pass by of us laughing.

I reach an arm over and place it on his shoulder, then continue my next story.

"So Amarille thought I was a thief and shot an arrow directly past my ear." I laugh. "So much for an anniversary surprise."

"Thank god she didn't go straight for your neck." Elliot laughs.

"I was very lucky I was not a bear."

A few more minutes pass with a few more cups drank.

"So, I tried to sneak out into the town to find a sauna and pay for some...lady favours?" Elliot says.

"How did that go?"

"Well." He snorts and laughs to himself. "My father was already there!"

We both howl like hyenas. Elliot leans his head on my shoulder as the two of us rock back and forth in the chairs trying to contain our bladders.

"You know, Elliot," I reach an arm over and tussle my hand in his hair, watching him pull away, "If I were to have another son, I wish he would be just like you!"

My eyes widen, and suddenly the laughing stops. I realize now what I have said and feel disgusted to even mention such a thing to him. His smile disappears into a look of pure confusion. I stand up from the table, barely able to feel my legs, but I get up and wobble towards the door, stopping to nearly throw up at the front door.

"Vesten!" Elliot comes up behind me and puts a hand on my back that I swiftly pull away from and fling my back against the door for support.

"I am sorry…soon we will part ways, and that will be the end of all of this."

"You don't mean that," he cries at me. "I think of you as a father—"

"I mean it all, Boy. This means nothing."

I rush out the door, for once ignoring the constant cries of Elliot behind me as he does not come outside and just cries inside. I feel a few tears around my face and look around for a sauna of some kind. Finally, I see one in the distance that I hobble and stumble towards, throwing up onto the snow the blue liquid which I had way too much of.

I reach the sauna and rush in, barely able to stand. I lean over the table and fling down a few gold pieces. The man is trying to take some of the coins.

"How many for a room?" He answers slowly to the point where I do not know if the booze is impacting my hearing.

"One," I say quickly, hoping not to stutter my words.

He takes a gold piece, and I pick up my coin purse, walking towards the saunas.

"Number five!" he calls out behind me.

I see the number five hastily through my vision and enter the sauna to the intense steam hitting my face. I reach around and fling off my belt, gambeson, and pants, throwing it all onto the floor without a care.

Now I take my stumbling naked body and splash the water into my face from the centre. There's a small pool at the centre with boiling water and a small wooden bench on the side that I fling myself onto.

Rubbing my eyes, I try to make sense of the constant stream of thoughts that pass through my head.

How could I be so stupid? Thinking that this fatherly relationship I am building with the young prince will in any way hold any form of validity. Once he is delivered back where he came from, that will be the end of it, his father will still have this ongoing war with Summerwind. I will have to fight against him. I have a child on the way at home that I am not there for, and now I am across the world bonding with a boy that holds such power and weight in the wars to come.

The worst part of this all isn't that I said I thought of him as a son, it's that, for a brief moment, I actually believed he could be.

Even if he thought I was his new father, it won't make a difference when I drop him off at Triumph. He will forget my name in a year. He won't remember my face, my sword, or anything I taught him. He won't care to remember my name.

He will become a triumphant king, overtaking his father and continuing this war. He will never ever go see or think about the man that helped him get there. He will have too many responsibilities.

He will find someone other than me.

I am a mere mercenary in his life that will hold no value once he moves on and goes straight back to royalty. Even with his father being a huge asshole, I would not be able to compete with a life of royalty and servants. All I have is my small family, and that is all I need.

I go to the centre of the sauna where the water is and begin to wipe away all the dirt and dried blood that covers my body, cleansing myself of the everlasting smell of travel and death.

My head still spins, but I take a moment to breathe while closing my eyes under the water, the heat reaching up and pressing against my face as I try to think about what my next plan of action will be. Maybe Elliot will forget all of this by morning, and we can blame it on the alcohol. Surely, he cannot think my words were genuine even though they were. It wasn't long ago I threatened to impale him with my blade.

I look over at my gear, which is covered in mud and travel much like myself. Bending over, I lift it all up to wash in the centre pool of water. The scented water does an incredible job at cleansing away the dirt and blood from my clothing and making my blade look good as new with its white steel reflecting in the water.

Finally, I figure I should head back and buy a room for Elliot and myself. Maybe I will pay extra gold and give him his own, buy him the company of someone so I do not have to worry about him thinking about me, his father figure that holds no grounds to a king.

I dry myself off with a towel and use a spare to dry off my gear, throwing everything on and feeling an uncomfortable stickiness that comes with still being wet and sweaty and attempting to put on clothing but pulling through anyway.

Slashing my sword back into its sheath with a hiss and snapping my belt back onto my waist, I wipe my hair from my eyes that I almost forgot was red behind the dirt that had built up and make my way outside of the sauna. I rush away from the man and barely nod at him, my legs still feeling weak but now actually able to walk somewhat properly without the need to stumble or throw up in the snow. It's a pitch-black night, and with my vision still hazy, I feel like I can barely see past the stream of snow that falls from the sky.

"Vesten," I hear a cold voice call out from behind me as if spoken into a tin can.

I turn to see a golden-striped guard, a helmet resembling that of a horse, and immediately I attempt to reach over and draw my sword but miss with my lack of depth perception. The Frozen Horse raises his fist, slamming it to the side of my face, knocking me unconscious.

15

THE FIRST TRIAL

Where am I? Why is everything dark? Why is there no light, and why is the only thing that feels like myself the voice inside my own head?

A bright flash brings me to my home. Amarille stands in front of me, looking younger, and smiling directly at me. Bringing my hands to hers, I look down at my hands and notice they aren't as scarred or taken by age as they should be. This had all happened in the past.

"The future seems bright then, doesn't it?" Amara looks towards my eyes, but I look away, trying not get lost in this trance.

"I suppose it does, beautiful," I reply without thinking, as if being controlled.

Why does this thing that has happened in the past feel real?

"Vest." Amara walks over to the window in our room and stares out towards the falling snow. "I understand you and Vesten Senior have not ended or met on the best terms but..."

"But what?" I say reluctantly, trying to look around but feeling trapped as if I am simply watching this thing from the past play before my own eyes. "What are you getting at?"

"Well, we are going to get married quite soon." She treads carefully with her words. "And I think it would be nice to invite your father since...your other one is no longer around."

"Amara," I try to speak.

"Just listen." She turns to me and grabs my hands. "Yes, you and Vesten Senior have not always gotten along, he was busy, and you were left by him on more than one occasion. I just—fear that he may not be around much longer, and with the loss of Dennen, maybe this is when he should come back into your life."

"He left, Amara." I place a hand against her cheek. "He made his decision to go to Eaforith. What makes you think he will come and reenter my life for a wedding?"

"I don't." She now places her hand on my cheek. "I just think it would be nice if he was invited to the wedding ceremony."

I laugh. "You want him to see us naked?"

"You know that is not what I meant." She smacks my arm. "For the ceremony of Aestas, it is customary that family is involved for good luck. We will do the Elvish wedding for me and well that can be just us...naked, as you say, for lack of a more romantic spin."

I find myself smiling and feeling warm on the inside, finally regaining control of this host body and touching her soft red hair and pointed ears. I shake my head to the side. I need to let her know this isn't real.

Just before I open my mouth to speak to her, I see another bright flash.

"Father!" Erron runs towards me and hugs me as I take my first few steps onto the dock outside of our house.

"Erron!" I once again do not have control over my body. "You are growing far too big when my eyes cannot see you!"

I lift him up into my arms. He must be no older than seven. Long hair that desperately needs cutting, and a smile that stretches ear to ear as he reaches in and gives me what just might be the biggest hug of all time.

I try to control my body, not to escape this vision that plays as if it's reality but to try and hug him tighter. No luck.

"He couldn't sleep last night," I hear the sweet voice of Amarille coming down the steps. "Far too excited to see you."

"And yourself?" I look into her green eyes.

"I could hardly sleep cause I was worried you would have lost an arm while sailing." She laughs with Erron as she walks close to us and pokes his nose.

"I missed you both, more than words can explain."

"Little Fox, go run off and find the new sword so father can see." Amara lifts him down from my arms, and he immediately smiles wide and runs towards the house.

"New sword?" I ask.

"It's wooden, he made it using some tree bark," she reassures me. "Best not keep him waiting."

I attempt to walk past her but am stopped by her hand on my chest.

"Yes?"

"*Froh'v*, forgetting anything?" She smirks at me.

I reach an arm over and bring her into a hug, kissing her lips, and bringing her close to me as tight as possible.

Once again, I try to break free of this illusion and hug her tighter… but once again, nothing.

Another bright flash, and my head is pounding from pain until eventually I am in Amara's and my room. We are younger once again, both of us naked, the glowing light from the orbs in the sky and candles illuminating our bodies.

She walks up to me and presses her soft body against mine, dancing with me while we listen to the sounds of the winter. My hands play with her hair and hers feel the scars along my back.

Hands of The Keeper.
Will of The Twins

Heart of Dormer.
Luck of Brenuin.

Give us warmth, love, strength, and luck.
Guide our hearts but fear never that of anything lesser than truth.

Tell me when the gods begin to watch it all.
And tell me why in your imperfections I only see stars.

For forever bound you will be mine, and for more I shall be yours.
Shut close the chapter of our previous lives and open up new doors.

Just us. Forever and Always.
Till the end of forever when all left is breath and blood.
For in yourself...I only see love.

THE POEM ENDS with us dancing back and forth in each other's arms. Now legally married to one another under Elven laws. I do not feel any different, only happier, I suppose, watching her light up immensely and bringing me in for a kiss. Still gently swaying back and forth to the music of the north.

Once again, I try to take control, tired of watching these visions that have come to pass play out in front of me. I try to speak, I try to squirm, move, and pray. The voice inside my head is the only thing that seems to know anything is outside of the ordinary as my body and voice call out to my wife the things I already said before.

Once again, I try to scream and shout. Feeling like an ethereal mind floating in nothing but a body that is not mine, every touch of Amarille feels real, but I know it is not. Almost like a siren trying to lure me into its grasp by using the things from my past over and over against me.

Finally, I am able to speak outside of the past.

"Amarille!" I now act shocked and surprised like how my inner subconscious is. I watch her not move her face and freeze in time. "Amarille! None of this is real! I need you to help me find out what this is!"

"Vesten." She places a hand to my cheek that I immediately grab back. "Why couldn't you save him?"

"What—"

Her hand feels as if it is burning. A sharp searing pain leeches itself into my skin as slowly she begins to turn to smoke and then disappears into nothing. I fall to my knees and see nothing but darkness surrounding me. A light is shining above me for which I cannot find the source, a circular glow around where I stand as if I am the only *thing* in this god awful nightmare.

I hear a loud clang behind me and turn around to see my sword impaled into the pure white ground. The darkness around still not revealing anything, and the blade is shining its white metal off the white light shining that looks like one of the orbs from the sky was placed overhead.

Still without any clothing, I feel immensely cold and don't know what to do. I stare at my sword for a few more moments until lifting it by its hilt and bringing it into my two hands. The moment I do, the metal fox eyes near the cross guard bleeds onto my body as I try to release the sword but can't.

I hear a loud screech behind me, and I turn to see a shadowy apparition. It's of Amarille holding a smokey version of the same sword I wield. I know it's supposed to be my wife, but it lacks anything that makes her inherently human. She wears long robes, and her green eyes are replaced with sunken black holes.

"Amara?" I whisper out to her but only hear a screech in return.

The shadowy figure running towards me with my blade attempts to slash at me. She jams her blade into my shoulder slightly, which seems to have magically placed my typical leather armour onto itself.

The pain feels as real as anything I felt outside of this hell. I bring my sword up and slash away at the demonic version of the woman I love.

A searing smoke emits from my left shoulder, and my sword still sprays blood everywhere from the fox's metal eyes.

I hear two more screeches from behind me and turn to see two more of the shadowy apparitions trying to steal my wife's likeness. They both run towards me with incredible inhuman speeds trying to slash away at me as, one by one, I cut them down.

Once again, to further solidify the nightmare, the blood rain begins.

Another two screeches behind me and two more in front, all running towards me and all of them attempting to slash away at me. I manage to block most of them off, my back leg getting cut by one of their unholy blades and causing me to bear through the searing pain.

I feel a hand reach my back shoulder, and I turn to slash, finding myself met with the face of Erron. He, however, does not look like one of those shadowy figures, though. He looks like my son.

I look down towards my body and notice I am no longer wearing my typical attire, but instead heavy metal armour with a golden streak straight through it and a helmet obscuring my view resembling that of a horse.

The mask disappears with Erron's squeal.

"Father?" he cries towards me. The metal armour slowly fades away piece by piece from me mirroring his body that almost looks like it is turning to dust. "You killed me?"

"Erron!" I yell even though he is right in front of me. Falling onto my knees and watching him mirror it, falling forward with his head now against my shoulder. My hand finds his hair that feels just as real as his tears that fall onto my now exposed shoulder. "I would never kill you, Little Fox, I promise."

He looks up towards me, now no longer wearing his face but that of Elliot's.

"But you did, father."

Another bright flash. This time with a feeling of falling as if I have fallen off a ship. My hair is flowing upwards in front of my eyes as the orbs are falling farther and farther away from me. My back slams into a snowbank.

I lift myself up. Now I am wearing winter clothing and no longer holding any kind of weapons. The frigid air of the far north pierces my skin. I take a few steps forward and look around at my surroundings.

In front of me, fireballs way off in the distance emit an orange glow as they dance around fields of blueberries. I am on top of a mountain in what I imagine is The Frost Meridiem, but I do not know where specifically.

I turn around and see something fly past my face with incredible speed, flapping away in the night and then turning towards me. A small stone pillar forms underneath the bird as it sits upon it.

"What is this?" I ask the mysterious small bird.

"Welcome to the gates of death," the younger female voice calls back to me.

"Am I dead?" I ask her.

"No, silly! Just at the gates!"

I walk closer to her, now seeing the small bird at the pedestal has a pendant around her neck that appears to be that of a flame quirk. I recognize the small bird. Sometimes, they would sing songs out front of the home in the mornings. She's a chickadee. "You're a…bird?"

"I am!" she chimes at me.

"Are you Lwo? Gatekeeper Of Death?"

"Lwo…well is kinda like me. Sort of like a silly extension of myself."

"So what are you?" I whisper to her.

"I am The Keeper!"

"You are…real? Have you been the one giving me these dreams?" I shiver and watch as she moves a wing, and suddenly, a fireplace emerges in front of myself.

"Nope!" She is rather blunt. "But I am the one keeping you here right now…haha. Keeper keeping you here."

"Can you release me, Keeper?" I try to ask as nicely as possible.

"I can…but not very easily."

"Why?" I fall onto my knees. "Why bring me atop this mountain I have never been? Why keep me in this state if for nothing?"

"Because you need to pass the trials," she says. "Three, and you have already passed one, yay!"

"Why the trials?"

"Because, Vesten, you need to prove your valour! I cannot just go giving away all of these lives to people!" I reach out and pet her head.

"I have heard of you," I whisper. "Not in this form, but my father told me of a transformed bird. I thought it was a story, but that bird is you isn't it?"

"I am everything now, Vesten." She opens her beak. "Now will you take part?"

"Yes, little bird. I will, and if I return to my father, I will let him know of your well-being."

"Good luck! I hope you do this for Elliot's sake!"

"Wait, how do you know of Eli—"

16

THE SECOND TRIAL

I take a deep breath as thousands of things are going on in my brain. I stare up towards the orbs piercing their rays onto my skin. I grasp the land underneath me and feel the deep grains of sand between my fingers. A few seagulls caw overhead, and the waves crash in front of me with saltwater pouring over onto my legs.

I lift myself up and look around this unfamiliar environment. It's a small sandy island in the middle of nowhere, no other land or any signs of civilizations as far as the eye can see.

I turn around to see a singular palm tree in the centre. I walk over to it and see Erron sitting down, drawing in the sand with a stick. He looks up to me and smiles, exposing his teeth and jumping around in excitement.

"Where are we, Little Fox?" I ask, rubbing the back of my neck which feels like it may be getting a sunburn.

"Home," he replies.

I look behind the palm tree towards the sea and see my sword, *Erron*, covered in blood and impaled into the sand.

"What is this?" I ask him.

"We are home." He smiles at me as I turn back around to look at him. A part of me knows I need to grab that sword. It calls out to me, and yet I feel the draw of this place. "Can you come sit? I have questions?"

I turn around once more and look at the sword but then walk back towards Erron and take a seat right next to him. We seem to be matching in torn up clothing suited for the blistering heat of wherever we are.

"What's the question, Erron?" I ask him, reaching out and touching his face with my fingers. His skin pushes back and reacts as if normal.

"Well actually I have a question about love." He smiles at me, still drawing in the sand.

I can't explain the feeling. I know this is a trial and yet it feels as if I could stay here. I'm not hungry nor thirsty, and if I am on death's door, maybe this is a direct link to talk to him again.

"What's the question?" I ask. "What are you drawing?"

"A ship," he says softly. "Like yours."

"Why a ship, son?"

"So we can leave, soon," he says.

"Do you remember how we got here?" I ask him.

"Nope, I remember waking up, and now we are here together."

"Alright." I cup his cheek with my palm. "So you have a question about love?"

"Yeah!" He gets excited and looks at me. "Like, I know I love you and mother, but I don't really know how it works with other people. I have a friend named Orieon in Aestas. Do I love him?"

"Oh, Little Fox. You won't really have to worry about any of that until you are a lot older. The most important thing you remember is that your mother and I love you. And that we hope you will always love us."

"Oh." He still smiles. "Well, I always love you two."

"And we always love you, too, Little Fox." I bring him closer and give him a kiss over the top of the head.

"Do you have any stories? Like the ones you tell when I pretend to sleep?"

"Pretend?" I laugh.

"Well, I need to hear how they end." He giggles.

"Sure, Little Fox, I have plenty I have always wanted to tell you."

* * *

Time does not seem to change, forever stuck with the orbs piercing down their lights, and the brightness of the daytime never leaving despite how long we stay here.

I tell Erron every fucking story I can think of. I do not know how this place works. I do not know if he is simply how my brain wants me to project him, but I know there is a slight chance it actually is him, and he is in the afterlife hearing me tell him these things.

I tell him about his mother, how she is expecting another child and how he would have been the best bigger sibling ever. I tell him about how I hope the next child is just like him, about how, no matter what, he will always be loved no matter how many children we have. That we will never forget him for as long as we live.

Days must've passed if time was working normally as it should. The time I just spent telling him about his mother's accomplishments was enough to fill a calendar. Then we moved onto things like growing up, the advice I had gotten from my father, and the countless life lessons I would hope he never had to experience while he was still breathing.

We walk together, hand in hand, around the entire small island, recounting tales and just enjoying seeing my son again.

I sit back down with him on the beach laughing. He scratches his arm, and I look over and notice his fire quirk tattoo. Maybe he had it before, but I never noticed until now.

"How long have you had that?" I ask him, knowing full well that he only got it in the few moments before he was burned alive.

"I don't know, just kinda showed up with me." He smiles at me.

"Do you have your quirk still?" I ask him. "In fact, snap your fingers."

"What?"

"Snap your fingers, it is just us on this island. No reason not to in the way I see it, no empires around, it's just us Little Fox."

I stand up and reach my arm out. He grabs it, helping himself onto his feet where we step in front of the palm tree towards the deep ocean in front of us.

"Did I ever tell you one of my fathers trained people with quirks?"

"No way! Really?" he says excitedly.

"Yeah, you would've loved him if you had the chance to meet him in your life," I say.

"Did he die before I was born?"

"Actually, Little Fox, you died before he and I could resolve any conflicts." I smile. "In a fucked up way, you are the reason he is back in my life."

My words don't seem to phase him the way they should. I hoped I would break this dream and have him admit he is truly my son's spirit and not just a figment of this trial inside my own mind or off in another reality.

He snaps his finger and a flame flickers over top of his fingertips, dispersing after a few seconds of his concentration losing focus.

"Oh my gods! Did you see that?"

"I did Little Fox." I turn around to see his drawing still etched into the golden sand. "In fact, wait here."

I walk over to where he was drawing in the sand, bending down and picking up the wooden twig he was using to draw, I walk over to him, then pass it over to him. He gives me a confused look.

"What is this for?" he asks, still very excited.

"Ignite it," I say quickly. "Ignite it and use it as a weapon."

"Are you sure this is allowed?"

"Who is going to stop us, Little *Froh'v*? Look around, it is just the two of us."

I rub my hand through his hair, messing it up and watching him back up smiling. Taking a deep breath and snapping his fingers, he hovers his stick above his finger, watching it catch immediately and ignite.

"Ah! Look, Father!" He waves it around in front of his face.

"Yes! Little fox, spin it around!" I yell, nearly jumping with him as he moves it around his body, for once not being afraid of his quirk but embracing it.

"I am the coolest!" he chants, dancing around with the fiery stick, repeatedly whacking invisible enemies in the air.

"That is right! Little Fox, no one can hurt you anymore! You are the greatest!" I walk over to him and bring him in close for a hug, making sure he keeps the open flame away from my face. I cry almost the second his hair reaches my nose. "I am sorry, Erron."

"For what?"

"I shouldn't have let them take you, I should have fought for you, I should have died for you, and a part of me feels like it has."

"No one is gone, we are right here. This is home."

"I know, Erron." I bring him in tighter for a hug. "I should have taught you to use it to your own advantage so you would forever be able to protect yourself. Maybe it was due to my hatred for my father that I shielded you from crucial information."

"I am protecting myself right now!" He takes a few steps back and shows me the stick that seems to not be burning away the wood and keeps the flame at the top.

"Yeah." I sniffle. "Yeah you really are, Little Fox." I look over towards the sword behind the palm tree. "I couldn't protect you."

"It doesn't matter…we are home now."

"You know I love you right, Little Fox?" I walk over to him and bring his forehead close to me for a kiss.

"Of course!"

"Good…then I am sorry," I say.

"For what?"

I ignore him and take a straight bee line towards the blade still sitting inside the sand.

"I promise," I yell back to my son without actually staring into his eyes. "I promise that home is wherever we will meet after this life. That there is more than this, if you are truly there listening. I promise I will see you again, Little Fox!"

I don't hear any response and turn away and don't see anyone there. The stick is stuck in the sand with a flame near the top. I look all around and don't see him anywhere. "I can only hope you have peace beyond the life you were given."

I walk over towards the white blade and grasp the hilt. The entire island and sky change to a dark hue, as if all of a sudden, it turned to night. The fires and lights from the sky are the only source of light as I turn around wielding the blade. The palm tree is gone, and the entire island is nothing but sand.

I feel something slash at my back leg, and I fall onto one knee. I turn around to see Erron holding a small blade in his hand.

"You don't want me to die again, do you?" he cries, looking at me.

"I would never wish such a fate on you, son." I hobble on my back leg despite the small stream of blood exposing itself from the skin. "But I know what this place is. I know you are not at peace while you are trapped here. I know that I love you, and I assure you that Amarille will know I saw you. Even if you are just a figment of my head."

"Father, please—"

I slash away at the apparition of Erron, watching black smog and smoke disperse from him until he falls into a pile of dust. I turn away from him and look up towards the sky where there doesn't seem to be anything changing. Even though I figure I've passed the trial, I am still stuck here.

"Father!"

"Father!"

"Father!"

I turn around to see the dust pile is gone, and in its place is a large fiendish creature. A tall, lanky, shadowy figure is in its place with three heads sprouting from its long necks resembling a dragon. At the end of each grotesque neck is the face of my son, all with a different expression. Happiness on the far left, fear in the centre, and sadness on the far right.

It moves like a snake, and its arms stretch out, slashing away at me. I fall back, nearly landing in the water at the other side of the secluded small island.

"I love you," the head on the left mimics.

"Please don't do this!" the head in the centre speaks.

"Why do you want me dead?" the final head exclaims.

"I know you are not him. I know my son is at peace and has been ever since the spire took his life in the darkness and smog that you imitate." I spit some blood on the ground. "And I know that I will find peace when you are destroyed for even daring to mimic him!"

I run towards them, the first head on the left diving towards me like a snake chomping away at a mouse. I spin around and slash away at its neck, my sword melting away with its acidic smokey blood as I am left with just my two hands against the remaining two heads.

"Please do not hurt me anymore!" the scared one chimes at me.

"Please, I don't want to leave you!" the final and most disturbing one mutters.

"Anything we do, we do for the advancement of ourselves!" I yell.

The heads both lunge at the same time now, both snapping and biting at me. One of them finds itself against my neck and tears a piece of my flesh out, spitting it out onto the sand as they fall back.

Once again, they lunge, only this time they both evade my attempt to punch. Flinging around my right arm and chomping away at the left while none of my brute force is able to stop them from ripping it off.

My arm gets spit out and flung behind them as I feel an immense rush of pain. Blood drains from my one arm, and my vision, within a few seconds, goes into a deep haze. I look up towards the two-headed demon and see both heads about to once again dive at the same time.

I wait until they lunge, and this time, I spin around the first head and grab its neck, immediately feeling the burn impact the layer of skin on my hand. I jam the open mouth into the other neck and watch as the entire apparition explodes into nothing but cloud and smog. My body is being pushed back once again, but this time, I land in the ocean. The water is deep and cold, and I look up towards the orbs in the sky and close my eyes. My blood is still draining from my missing arm.

I am barely able to see through my eyelashes before the water opens and pulls me directly under. My lungs feel collapsed as slowly all light fades away and farther and farther into the depths I go. My arm feels numb, and my brain soon follows suit until finally there is nothing but black and darkness.

A part of me thinks this is just where I will stay, forever living over and over in these limbo situations until I go mad and am met with death. Nothing but eternal mental and physical pain forever.

17

THE FINAL TRIAL

I take a deep gasp of air, and suddenly I am in my bed. The warmth now fades in, and the first thing I do is look over and confirm that I still have my limbs.

I look around my room, which looks to be normal. Even some of the wooden planks are just as crooked and splintered as when I first placed them down. The main difference is the landscape outside is gone. Looking out my windows, I don't see the sea or trees. I only see pure bright white light that almost pierces through and gives way to the entire atmosphere of the house, but somehow it doesn't.

I get out of bed and walk out of the room, not wearing much except my typical casual clothing. This time, there is no bloody sword anywhere that calls me to it. I just feel the same nostalgic feeling I always did whenever I would step foot into Amarille's and my home.

I walk out of the bedroom and close the door behind me. Still, everything seems normal except for the outside. Despite it being bright white, it doesn't call to me. It gives me a feeling of uneasy dizziness the longer I stare out, hoping to see anything.

"Hey *Froh'v*," Amarille calls out from in front of me, rocking a very young Erron in her arms. "How did you sleep?"

"Had a crazy amount of dreams, but I'm better now." I walk over behind her and wrap my arms around her arms to press my hands against hers.

"I have a surprise for you." She sounds secretive. "But it can only be once this little *Froh'v* is asleep."

As if small Erron heard her call, he stops crying and goes into a sleep. I suppose part of realizing this is all a sequence of dreams is that, in reality, he never would have stopped crying that quickly in real life.

She places him gently back down into the crib next to the ongoing fire and takes my hand, bringing me back where I came from in the bedroom.

"What is this big secret?" I ask.

"Just come here, quietly *Froh'v*!" She continues to pull me over and now places me underneath the wooden shower head. "I haven't seen you in a while and quite simply, we need more time together."

She pulls the rope, and immediately the hot water pours over my head and onto my nice casual clothing.

"Darling! Couldn't you have just asked me to rem—"

"Shhh!" She hops into the shower with me, making sure she doesn't trip over the tiles that lead up into the bedroom that protects the room from any water damage. "I missed you!" Even her whispers sound demanding and sweet.

"I—" I realize this is all simply an illusion. It is my brain showing me everything it remembers from this memory, and yet I do not want it to end. Why would I? For once there is no death or destruction. It's just the woman I love and a shower. "I missed you too, beautiful."

She helps me remove my clothing and toss them aside until, finally, we are both naked and pressed against each other in the water, just enjoying each other. Her belly still has a few of the stretch marks and scars from her pregnancy, but I still think everything about her is perfect. After all, I'm one to talk with the amount of assorted scars I have across my body.

I bring her lips in for a kiss and press my hand against her face. I enjoy the feeling of brief calm with her as the water pours over us both, and as she looks at me, I feel my stomach flutter as if we are young again. Her piercing green eyes and countless freckles smile up at me as I bring her in once for a kiss. Despite us looking a lot younger since this dream is when Erron was first born, she still looks just as beautiful in this memory as she does in my reality. Still makes me feel the same butterflies and everlasting glow.

"I have so much I want to tell you," I whisper to her, pushing her now wet hair behind her large elven ear.

"Later," she whispers back. "First, just kiss me."

She kisses me for a few more seconds before finally sliding her hands down my chest and onto my stomach, looking up at me before walking out of the shower and lying down on the bed.

I walk over, not caring about the water dripping onto the wooden floor, and lean over and on top of her, pressing my body against hers and feeling her hand reach behind my neck. She brings me in once more for a kiss.

A few minutes or maybe hours later, we both are still lying in bed together enjoying each other's company just as I remember.

I wake up once more as if nothing happened, and I was just sent into the cold sea. My right arm desperately reaches over and frantically searches to assure my left arm is still in its proper place, attached to my body.

This time, I jolt out of bed and walk out of the bedroom ignoring the same white light that shines through the windows. I see Amarille rocking Erron back and forth in her arms, everything repeated from yesterday or whenever the last dream sequence was. How many times did I fall for it? Did I spend all of that time reliving this day over and over, and this is the first I remember? Or is this quite simply the day after?

Why does it feel like so much time has passed when the only memory I have is that of the same one that played for me yesterday. I knew it was a dream, and yet every time I would still choose to step into the shower with my wife and go straight to the bed with her. How come, right now, I understand that this is all repeating?

"Amarille?" I say to her as I walk closer to her.

"Yes, *Froh'v*?" She turns to me smiling.

"How long have we done this?"

"Done what? We have put Erron to bed—"

"That is not what I mean, Amarille," I nearly yell now.

I feel the sweat covering my body and dripping from my forehead. Clearly, she can see I am distressed and puts Erron down the second he goes straight to sleep.

"*Froh'v*? What is the matter?" She walks up to me and presses the back of her hand against my forehead. "Are you feeling okay? We should head back to bed."

"Amarille, I need you to listen to me, okay?" I ask.

She nods her head, but her eyes still widen, and she stares at me like I have gone insane.

"What is it?"

"I have lived this day. I do not know if this is the second or the hundredth, but I need to break the cycle."

"Darling, I probably have said this before to you, but you sound mad!" She laughs. "Feel my face."

She reaches down and lifts up my hands to press against her cheeks. "I am really here! This isn't a dream of any kind!"

"Amarille," I whisper, bringing my forehead to hers and pressing against it. "I am dead, this isn't real, and I know this sounds insane, but I need you to try and understand me, please. You're the smartest person I know, and I cannot have you not believe me right now."

She moves her head back away from mine and takes a minute, tilting her head at me before lifting herself up slightly to reach eye level and planting a kiss on the tip of my nose.

"Come to bed my *Froh'v*."

"Fuck!" I yell, looking over at Erron, who doesn't even wake up at the scream a few feet away from him. "Amarille, I am scared without you! I feel lost without you! I need you to please understand I am lost here and need you to let me think of a way out."

"Vesten." She laughs once more. "The only way out of anything is out that front door, and I don't imagine you are going to leave Erron and I alone anytime soon."

I look up at her, immediately having the realization. I look over towards the front door just past the fireplace and walk over to it. Opening it with one hand on the doorknob and looking out towards the endless amount of white, I hold onto the doorframe and feel where the step normally should be in front of the door, but my leg just passes right through. As if the entire house is floating in nothing, and if I walk out, I will fall directly past it.

I just stare down into the abyss of white that is there below me. I feel Amarille come up behind me and wrap her arms around my stomach.

"Darling, promise you will never leave me," she whispers into my ear.

She remains just as pure and beautiful as anytime I get to lay eyes on her, and she stares directly into my eyes. There is no snake-like creature for me to face here...just the woman I love that I never want to leave.

"I do everything I must for our family. I swear I will see you soon."

"So stay," she whispers to me. "Forever live this life where nothing bad has happened or is going to happen. Forever Erron will remain young and so will we, forever in love and alive."

"Everything happens for a reason, beautiful." I feel a tear fall from my face as I press my hand one more time against her face. Gently rubbing my thumb against her freckles and wiping away her tears in the process. "There is someone out there in a lot of danger, and right now, he needs my help."

"If that is the case, *Froh'v*, go and help him," she cries back after seeing me cry.

I know she isn't real. I know she doesn't understand a word I am saying since she lives deep inside my mind. Hearing her, however, tell me I should go chase after this boy even if it technically is my own subconscious telling me, is something that makes me feel like an entire weight has been lifted off my shoulders. I can only hope that back in my reality she will be this understanding when I tell her in person.

"For Erron," I whisper to her.

I lean in and kiss her before leaning my entire body backward and out the door frame and house. I fall deeply into the white abyss. She very swiftly fades from view as I freefall in the air and close my eyes. My hair moves directly in front of my face and the home slowly moves farther and farther away from my vision.

I am coming, Elliot.

18

WHO WE ARE

Is this another dream? My feet dangle beneath me, and my arms are bound to one another by rope as I dangle from the ceiling. Blood pours out from my face and body into the pool of red liquid below me.

My vision finally comes back to me fully. I don't know how long I was out, but I know a few days must have passed in my trial. I stare down at my body dangling below me and wiggle my toes to assure I still have control over everything. Looking up, I move my fingers as well.

I do not know why I am covered in so much of my own fresh blood. Did they torture me while I was unconscious? What would they gain from that? Was I awake enough that they would deem me 'alive' enough to try to gain information from me?

I taste blood pooling inside my mouth and spit it towards the wooden door in front of me, a door which, much like myself, is covered in blood. I look around this cold empty cellar, concrete floors, walls, and a ceiling. I imagine that I'm not the first person to find himself here. Some of the dried blood even seems to be a different colour, meaning a variety of races were tortured here as well. My bare chest bleeds onto my pants and then onto the floor.

A single candle just next to the door is lighting the small enclosure just enough that I have good enough visibility to realize the door is my only escape. I don't know if I am already in Triumpth or if I am quite simply somewhere far away from Slimhixe.

I hear footsteps in front of me and lift my head towards the door, spitting once more at it before it swings open and two frozen horses walk in. Their shiny armour is freshly cleaned as the pungent smell of fruits overtake my sinuses.

"Oi, lads, he is finally awake," the first one chuckles, calling up the staircase before closing the door behind him. "Don't worry fellas, I will handle him."

"Where is Elliot?" I waste no time.

"The prince you kidnapped? I imagine being sent back home by our righteousness. Not that you will be alive long enough to see him again."

"Why?" I close my eyes and tilt my head down. "Why not just kill me then?"

"Kill you?" He scoffs. "Wouldn't be very honourable of me to kill you. You still have to stand trial and answer to your crimes."

"What. Fucking. Crimes?"

The frozen horse walks up to me, his helmet's long snout resembling a mare nearly pressing against my forehead. He takes a step back and removes it, revealing a bald head and charred face. He clenches his fist a few times against his palm before swinging out and slamming against the side of my face with his gauntlet. My entire body swings with the force of the fist.

"You will be hanged." He brings himself close to my face smiling. "For treason against the empire…although I guess if I say you fought back, I could stab you. You got a mighty fine blade upstairs."

Another quick, cold, metallic punch to my gut, and I cough blood out onto his face. He wipes it away and smiles at me as if it's pleasant to him.

"I guess the same could be said for the prince. You and he are in very similar circumstances at the moment."

I look up at him, trying to mask the desperation in my eyes with anger.

. . .

"If you so much as—"

Another quick punch to my face.

"You won't be around much longer to have any say." He chuckles. "See you around, kidnapper."

He walks out and closes the door behind him before I can say anymore to him.

I continue to dangle, new blood pouring onto my body as nothing changes. The candle continues to flicker, and time seems to pass only measured by the thoughts inside of my head.

There is no source of daylight or nightlight. I feel like a few hours have passed since my last interaction with the bald, frozen horse, but I can't tell. My mind feels drowsy, as if I haven't slept for a few days, so maybe that's a sign that it's getting late in the day.

A small breeze flows past my hair with the sound of flapping wings. A bird flies past my ears with a ghostly smoke following the trail left behind her. The small pudgy bird lands directly on top of the candle, not igniting but becoming the flame.

"Congratulations, Vesten!" she chirps at me.

"Keeper?" I mumble, staring directly up at her. The feathers completely ignite in flames as her head makes the sudden sporadic movements associated with a bird. "Is this another trial?"

"Nope!" She sounds excited. "You have passed all your trials!"

I feel the ropes binding my arms to the ceiling glow brightly as a flame flickers from the top and makes its way down the entire thing. I squirm, trying to avoid any burning, flailing my arms back and forth with my body until realizing it isn't piercing or hurting my skin. Only burning away the rope and causing me to fall onto the cold cement.

My body immediately becomes winded, and my breath feels scattered with endless wheezing. I press my palms against the floor, trying to lift myself up and making it a quarter of the way before falling back onto my face. A spray of blood spurts out from my mouth and towards the bottom of the metallic candle where, near the top, the chickadee perches.

A few sparks form on her body like an untempered fireplace until the sparks become more and more frequent. The sparks now fling off of The Keeper's body and onto my back, finding themselves sinking in my skin one after one with an orange glow accompanied right after.

I feel the sparks flow throughout my body, an orange glow radiating off each of them as they make their way into my fresh wounds and sealing them off. The blood no longer drips from them, and a few scars that match the ones already on my body form.

I now press my knuckles and fists against the floor and lift myself up with my body, no longer feeling that exasperated weakness of the torture but now more like myself. My foot flings out from underneath me to my chest, and I lift myself onto my two legs. Wiping the sweat away from my forehead, I reach my arm out to pet the flaming bird with my fingers.

The flames, like the ones that scorched the ropes, do not hurt me.

"Thank you," I whisper.

"Your life is yours to complete, silly."

She opens her beak wide, I suppose, trying to mimic a human smile.

"Why me? Why was I chosen to do the trials?"

"Because *the red rain* is yet to happen, Vesten."

I feel my heart drop to my stomach with her words. The red rain that has plagued my nightmares for as long as I can remember surely must have already happened. In my head? In the trials? It must be over!

"What do you mean the red rain has yet to happen? Surely it is just in my head?"

"Oh, shoot! I have said too much."

With a flash, she fades away, leaving me in the room alone. A candle is left in her place, and scorched rope lies behind me.

I shake my head, trying to remember my objective. Elliot needs my help.

I swing the door open behind me and tuck myself down onto my knees to make as little noise as possible, moving my way up the concrete stairs until finding myself out in a small room surrounded by a few of the frozen horses. This must be a hut for wines and meats, and I have been trapped in the wine cellar along with the other poor souls that have come before me to await the king's justice.

There are two people sleeping to my left in single beds, one in a bed to my right, and one larger bed directly in front where I see the bald man from earlier resting. I stare out the window above the wooden door at the front of the wooden hut and see it is pitch black in the night. Crouching closer and staring out the window, I notice the orbs are still high in the sky, meaning night is close to just beginning.

I look over to my right and see a small chest, a blade poking out from a small black blanket that is being used to cover the entire thing. I gently lift up the blanket to reveal my sword, sheathed, and reflecting its white glow as the light from the orbs pierce into the window.

I lift it up and unsheathe it gently so the hiss of the blade revealing itself is nothing more than a slight whisper. Standing up onto my feet, I make my way over to the first bed. Lifting it over the man's neck like a saw, I slide it through effortlessly like butter. Then I make my way to the next bed, and the next one. Before I reach the third one, the bald man gargles blood, and for a moment, I almost fear that it is going to wake him up.

I walk over to him and stand above him, this time with my hilt slamming it down and against his nose. He squeals and throttles around, trying to get back up before I bring him back down and press the blade against his neck.

"Where is Eli?" I ask.

"The fucking boy?" He removes his hands from his nose, revealing that it's crooked and deformed and covered in blood. "Go fuck—"

I slam my hilt once more against his face and then slide the white blade over his neck. This time a slight orange hue glows from it but not nearly at full capacity.

"You know, the boy was with me when I got this sword." I chuckle. Sawing it back and forth without making contact with his neck. I watch it glow brighter and brighter. "He didn't even know that once this blade reached full hue, it would shock the entire person like a thunderbolt straight from the gods' hands."

"Wait, wait!" He pushes his head down as far as he can into the bed and stares up at me. "I just take orders."

"And how many other people in the basement were orders?" I tilt my head. "Now look, I am running out of patience because that boy is in a lot of danger, so either you tell me where he is, or I send a shock through your body so charged up that you fry like an over-burned slab of meat."

He turns and looks up into my eyes, my sawing back and forth finally coming to a halt when the blade cannot glow any brighter, resembling a slab of metal that has just been taken out of the coals of a blacksmith's forge. Upon first glance, you would probably expect this once-white blade to burn instead of shock.

"I do not know where the boy is!" He tries to defend himself.

"Then you are no use to me." I raise the blade above my head, watching him lift his hands up in defense.

"Wait!" He brings his hands to his face crying. "Fine, fine, you fuck! He is at Boneshiver! East of here!"

"Thank you!"

I bring the blade down and slice straight through him with bright purple lightning bolts finding their way across the entire room. One of them even shooting towards the glass window above the door and shattering it to pieces before, finally, the room goes silent and the blade turns white.

I walk over to the chest, now covered in small glass shards, and lift up the lid, revealing my clothing and gear. Putting all of it on, I finally walk out into the cold. Taking a quick note of my surroundings, I see that there are no horses.

"Vesten!" I hear the young voice behind me.

"Keeper," I say rather tamely, looking at the chickadee perched on the broken window. "What now?"

"I am kinda late giving this to you. I thought Amarille should see it first!"

A flame spits out a small pouch to the ground.

"Wait, you spoke to Amara?" I shake my head. "Wait what did you mean about the red rain?"

"Can't say, otherwise I would have to. . ." She coughs. "**Temper my blade in your heart,**" she mimics my voice. "Goodbye, Mr. Vesten."

"Goodbye, little bird." I rub the top of her head.

"Oh, right." She giggles and opens her beak. "The word is haste!"

"Wait, what—"

With a bright orange flash and a sizzle of flames, she disappears, leaving just the pouch sitting in the snow.

What a fucking confusing bird.

I lift it up and notice it has something tucked into it. Opening it, a small stone falls down from the letter and into my hand.

For a brief second, the stone glows a symbol I cannot place that looks to be in a new language. The glow fades away and appears on the backside of my palm. I drop the stone to the ground.

The word is haste.

"Haste?" I whisper out to the nothingness of the snow. The only thing new is I seem to look mad. I try to think of what The Keeper meant by that.

What is the elvish word for haste? I try to think back to the alphabet.

"Ahex—" I cough and look up to the sky. "**Ahexnal.**"

When I look back down, I see a horse standing in front of me. Only this horse is not a simple mare. It has matte black skin and a white mane. Looking into its eyes, I can tell they're not that of any creature but of a universe. Stars shining in a cosmos that seems to continuously float.

I go to the back of the mare and see a bright blue handprint that glows much like its eyes. In the starry hand is the word "Amarille." And I realize it's the hand of my wife. I bring my hand up over it to feel the outline of hers. The glowing symbol from the stone leaves the back of my hand and engraves the horse a new handprint, my own, that reads "Vesten, The 2nd."

I smile and hop on the back of the horse. There's no saddle, but the horse feels designed to be perfectly comfortable. I recognize it from stories from a long time ago, some of which may be collecting dust back at home. It's an *eternity mare*, a horse made to never tire, eat, sleep, and come back to a command which I suppose, for me, is the elvish word for haste.

I thought these horses were just as long gone as dragons themselves.

I drop my smile and hold onto the back of its mane.

"Come on, girl...let's go get the prince."

19

THE HEART OF THE KINGS CAGE

ELLIOT

I cough up blood and look down at my bruised hands tied to a wooden chair I do not recognize. I'm in a place I do not recognize that appears to be a large tent surrounding me. The chair sits on the cold, now-melted grass from the few candles in each corner.

I try to shake away and tilt the chair but hear a loud clang of metal shackles that bind the chair to a post leading up its back. A post I can just barely feel if I lean my head all the way back in its place. My hands are shackled by the same metal chain that's wrapping around all the way down and around my feet.

I scream, but no one answers. Who captured me? Why would they ever think about capturing a prince and keeping him bound to a chair? Where's Vesten?

The tent opens in front of me and in walk two guards, only...I recognize them. Frozen Horses with their armour resembling stallions glistening behind the three orbs. Helmets shroud their faces but, judging from the more slender physique of the guard on the left, it must be a male and female duo that have come to save me.

"Oh thank the fucking gods." I smile at them. "Did my father send for you two?"

"He did," the male voice coldly calls out like a tin can. "He sent for us, Little Prince."

The first guard pulls out a knife from behind his back with the pale expression of the helmet staring down upon me. My smile fades away almost immediately when I look down at my binds. If they were going to set me free…*they would have pulled out a key.*

The cold-voiced guard jams his knife into my leg. I let out a howling scream before the female walks around the chair and shoves a rope into my mouth, pulling my neck back with it as my eyes cry and warm blood pours onto my right leg. The final knot is tied around my neck as I lean my head over and see the cold knife still lodged into my leg and plunged through to the wooden chair.

My leg still oozes blood. I let out the largest scream I can possibly manage in hopes someone comes for me. I look up at the tent which has its flaps closed shut, praying that after a moment Vesten will walk in with his glowing sword and save me from this pain.

I fling my head back with the pain searing into my leg like hot coals still orange and molten. The taller guard slams the back of his hand against the side of my face, and I feel the coarse metal of his gauntlets piercing into my skin. He slaps me so hard the chains are the only thing that keep me from falling over.

The female one from behind removes the gag and flings my head forward. Blood and fragments of my teeth spit onto my lap as I cry.

"I bet you think we are from Slimhixe," the female one scoffs. "We are from Summerwind, Little Prick."

"Why?" I whisper while gritting my teeth together as the pain never leaves my leg.

"Your father took our daughter from us, Little Prince." The male one removes his helmet and stares into my eyes. "I look forward to taking his kin from him."

Another swift blow to the back of my head from the female bandit, and my vision sees stars. Flashing orbs in my vision until finally everything comes back to me, but my head pounds behind me. I feel some blood slide its way down my back and into my tunic, but it doesn't seem to hurt as much as the knife still lodged into my leg.

"Please," I cry out, coughing some blood out onto myself. "Gold, fame, anything that you need!"

The male one goes down onto one knee and forces my head up with his bloody gauntlet. My eyes match his through the blurriness of my sight. He places the horse-shaped helmet he was just wearing over my face.

"I want my daughter back, you fucking twat!"

Once again, he punches me, this time the helmet obscuring when the blow will hit and the entire horse-shaped metal mask spinning a few times around my smaller head as I cry into the echoing helmet. One more swift punch upwards towards my chin, and the helmet flies off and into the dead grass.

"There is a large bounty on your head in Slimhixe now. Even your father is auctioning the whole thing off as some kind of closure."

Why would he do that? Why would he encourage my own death instead of prioritizing my safe rescue back to him like any other father would do?

"Where is my mother?" I mumble in pain with my ears still ringing from the helmet.

"Oh? Ya did not hear? She is long gone." The male one laughs to himself. "Traitor to your capital…pity I suppose…would have loved to hear her scream."

I lash out as much as I can. The pain in my leg disappears for a brief few seconds as adrenaline courses through my veins, and I shake my entire body hoping the chains will break with a miracle. I do feel the one shackle on my right arm jitter and shake a lot more than the left but think nothing of it and get punched again directly in the eye.

My vision is black on one side with only one eye open, I lean my head down towards the knife still lodged into my leg. My breath shallows. I do not know if I'm going to pass out or simply die where I sit, but nevertheless, the two guards gag me once more and leave.

I try to look out of the tents' flaps once they open but see nothing except for the bright white lights of the winter blinding my only working eye. Left alone to sit with the excruciating pain in my leg, I shake more violently than the last time. I try to think about what

Vesten would do in this situation, but that only leads to more sadness as I realize he is probably long dead by now.

The moment they captured me inside of the bar, I imagine they would have taken him out to the sidewalk and beheaded him for the sake of the king. If I was captured by Summerwind guards, that must mean they will eventually take me directly south, back to the warmth where they will either hang me or keep me as some kind of bargaining chip in their war. A war I had no choice but to be brought up into being a part of.

What's so fucking fucked about this whole matter is those Summerwind guards want me dead for the death of their daughter. Something at the hands of my father just like Vesten's son. Only Vesten was able to forgive or at least realize I truly had no say in the ideals of Slimhixe. I wonder how many other people had their children or loved ones taken from them at a spire…all while believing a young prince could in any way give them closure. I did not want anyone to be burned at the spire or tortured. I just wanted the affection of a father who was so caught up in the drink and in the lay of women.

My vision clouds around itself in a thick, black smog, and I realize soon I will pass out. I try to shake my head again to rekindle my thoughts. One last push of adrenaline that could potentially get out of me is the only shot I have between being lost in the wilderness of an unknown place…or a rope around my neck.

I think about my mother…why would she become a traitor to the empire? Maybe she argued over my safety due to the new rule that even my own damn people can put an end to my life and find themselves in riches rather than their own blood.

I think about all the songs she used to sing to me when I was little…pretending neither of us could hear the whores beyond the walls as she sat with me waiting for my father to be done with his pleasure-driven hobbies. The song about the owl singing to his love the bear, the song about the bard and his love for a dragon who liked to read. Everything was so much more simple then.

I miss that feeling of safety with her hand inside of my hair and her soft voice as she would sing me to sleep. It all seems so distant now, like a faded memory.

I shake in my shackles and let out a yell into the gag, feeling the blood building up inside my mouth and onto the rag, I try to spit some of it away but fail. With my right shackle feeling loose, I look over and notice it's not as tight as the one leaving a purple ring of bruises along my left wrist.

I shake and pull as much as I can, trying to squeeze my more-slender hand and wrist through the metal bar. My wrist gets through the majority of the cuff. Now I just have to pull my hand through in order to be free. I pull and pull as hard as I can, trying to somehow move my hand through the bar, but I fail. The rigid inside of the shackles splinter along my skin and tear away the flesh from the skin of my hand. Scraping my hand through, it covers itself in some blood as most of the skin has skid away from the cuffs.

With my right hand free, I reach over and undo the cuffs on my left. Hitting the emergency lever that I should never have been able to reach, I reach my hands behind my back to untie the gag. Finally, I get the knots undone and the rag falls forward with a waterfall of blood that had built up inside of my mouth, pouring all over my legs and the knife that impales itself into my leg.

I reach down with my free left hand and unshackle the first cuff on my left leg. Now looking over at the knife in my leg, I know I will need to pull it out in order to free the final limb from being bound.

I take a few deep breaths, swallowing them with each new huff in order to prepare for the pain. I take the blood-covered rag that was used to gag me earlier and shove it in between my teeth so I do not bite my own tongue off. Sweat pours from my forehead and body as if every pore is anticipating what's about to come.

I reach over and grasp the knife gently, the mere slight movement being enough that I scream into the rag while tears fall down from my face. I count to three in my head and try to think back to the songs mother used to sing to me. Humming the words of *The Canary & Deer* through the gag before pulling the knife out with as much force as I can. First feeling it go through the chair with some splinters finding their way into my skin. I have to stop halfway through due to not being strong enough to pull it all out at once. I continue humming this time, louder and more aggressive as I scream into the rag once more and lift the blade from my leg, holding it in the sky and throwing it off to the side.

I reach down and quickly undo the lever of the shackle, so my entire body is finally free at last. I pull the rag out from my mouth and begin to wrap it around my leg as it oozes some more blood everywhere. Looking down towards the open wound as I tightly wrap it, I nearly throw up on myself, trying my best not to gag or make any noise above the previous muffled screams.

I stand up on both legs, trying my best not to fall over and using the chair as balance. My right leg is not strong enough to support my entire body. I use my left leg for the majority of the trip, hobbling my way out of the tent and into the cold air that feels especially nice on my sweaty face and body.

I look around and see the camp that seems to have no signs of anyone, let alone those two guards that tried to cripple me earlier. I hobble behind the tent and out wherever that way leads. Coming across a slightly taller cobblestone structure, I realize I was trapped inside of a broken-down castle as opposed to a camp out in the open. Meaning I have to find the front gate in order to fully make my way safely out into the night.

I follow the wall as quietly as I can while mostly walking on one leg and using the cobblestone as a sort of cane to keep myself balanced properly. Finally seeing the front gate where two people stand guard, I look around for a rock of some sort on the ground or lodged into the wall.

Finding a small piece of stone along my feet, I bend over while biting my tongue due to the pain. Throwing it over and towards a tent behind them, it makes a loud clang, and the people move away from the gates.

I make my way closer and closer until taking a few deep breaths and feeling my heartbeat out of my chest. Only...something isn't right.

The flags are not Summerwind, they're the Slimhixe insignia, meaning the two people torturing me were not simple spies like I thought them to be. It means they were my father's men.

"Got ya, boy!" I hear a grunt from behind me and see a new guard on a horse donning Slimhixe colors jumping off of his stallion and running for me.

"No! Wait! I am the prince! My father is the king!" I try to reason.

The guard kicks my bandaged bloody leg, and I fall like a pile of rocks onto my face and stomach, turning myself over and seeing the guard in the darkness stand above me smiling.

"Who do you think sent us to capture you?"

20

NO TIME FOR CAUTION

"Come on, girl!" I slam the reins down towards Boneshiver where Elliot is being held.

It's north-East from where I am now. Following the ocean all the way up is the best and fastest route to get to him before nightfall.

I have no plan for when I get there. I figure trying a diplomatic approach at first might work in order to get Elliot out without any harm coming to him or putting his life in danger. Lucky for me, the orbs are just beginning to rise and shine their lights over top the snowy terrain and out from the water.

The winter air chills my exposed fingertips as I repeatedly slam the reins down to make the horse go as fast as physically possible. The chilled wind against my ears and face causes them to turn a shade of red. Every few seconds, I make sure to breathe some warm air into my palms and onto my face to try to fend off the frostbite.

I've never actually been to Boneshiver, only knowing what most sailors do of the landmark location of Slimhixe. It's an old, small stone castle that fell quickly to the war when one single boat came and overtook it. The people on the boat didn't even stay long, a simple show of power to Slimhixe at the start of the war that showed they were not some impenetrable border.

I wonder why they took Elliot there. He's the prince, after all, so why not just take him up to Triumpth where his father is? It would have not only been a shorter travel time but also much, much easier than taking him to such a private location, unless...well, unless the guards were given different orders from the king. Which would mean Elliot is in a lot more danger than anticipated. Nothing is worse than a king who doesn't even care for this own bloodline.

For a brief moment, the idea crosses my mind that I might just be too late when I arrive, that he may just be a corpse and left to die alone in the cold away from his home. Would I just go back to Amarille and have to tell her the reason I was so late coming to see her was that I failed to protect the prince of the other side? Would she understand the sadness that would overtake me if I lost him? I immediately denounce the thoughts when I remember I have no time to think like this. Elliot is a smart kid. He will say or do something to either escape or talk his way out of death. At least for the time being.

My face is getting exponentially more and more chilled by the constant travelling north towards the camp, but I never stop. I'll never be able to live with myself if I'm a minute too late, if I arrive and his body is still warm, and the guards are packing their things to take his head to the capital for their sum of the reward. I continue to push on for Elliot.

* * *

FINALLY, after the seemingly endless horse ride leading towards Boneshiver, I see it off in the distance. Standing tall despite being broken in more than one corner and just barely keeping intact the four walls; it still looked impressive. It's an abnormally important landmark in the war between the two powerhouses of Verenden that has been relegated to simple textbook knowledge.

I finally slow down the horse and let her take some well-deserved, huffing breaths. With my sword strapped along the side of my body, I place one hand on the hilt and the other with fingers wrapped around the reins.

The cobblestone structure appears much larger the closer I ride up towards it. Two shiny-armoured frozen horses stand out in front of the wide open entrance, standing post. With long swords held at their sides and breath shooting from the masks' imitated nostrils, they sway side by side, appearing to talk to each other about something rather humorous, at least according to their hearty laughter.

I fling myself off Ahexnal and slowly approach them.

"Excuse me! You two!" I yell, waving my right arm around in the air, knowing very clearly they can see me.

"Halt!" one of them chirps up as I try my best to fake huffing like my horse. "What brings you here?"

"I am a messenger from Triumpth, sent here to deliver a message to your higher ups."

They both take a second and stare at me as I fake a smile ear to ear, looking my body up and down and probably noticing some of my own blood stained into the fabric, barely exposed by the torch that stands beside them.

"What's a messenger doing with a sword that fancy?" the guard on the left asks. "Or an…eternity mare?"

I drop my smile and shrug my shoulders.

"You two are right. I have no time for this," I say.

In one fell swoop, I hiss open my blade and grasp it in both hands while dropping the reins. I'm about to swing at one of the guards when they raise their hands up in the air.

"Wait!" the one on the left pleads without even trying to go for his blade. "Just…walk in. We do not mean to give away our lives for them."

I tilt my head and simply stare at them both while holding the sword. The guard on the right nudges the other, and they both slowly walk away from the front entrance and towards the darkness I had just ridden in from.

A part of me ponders the idea of simply killing them for the sake of safety, but I realize if they truly wanted a confrontation, they would have just ran into the front entrance screaming for help.

I bring my sword back down to its sheath on the left side of my body.

"Go, girl!" I hit the horse's back to make it gallop away.

Taking a torch from the front, I bury the head into the snow so it extinguishes.

I now slowly crawl and make my way into the compound. Immediately, I hug the broken wall on the right side and use it to stay in complete darkness while making my way throughout the compound until I know where Elliot is. So far, it seems like I am having less than no luck. Every one of the tents look the same greyish colour, matching the walls. Everywhere I look, I see something I've already seen or, at least, think I've seen. Nothing stood out.

I think back to the dream, to Amarille, and the constant desire to forever be with her. The pulling sensation of the dream keeps me, even now, wishing to be back in that state of mind.

"Please! I am the queen!" I hear a scream from out of the centre tent. "You cannot do this!"

I look over to see a woman with tired eyes being carried away by a male and female guard, kicking and screaming at them, cursing out their names in vain as she is brought to a wagon. The wagon doors throw themselves open with a loud crack on either side as a larger man cackles his way out.

"Oh, my darling dearest, Celacine," the king smirks. "A shame you will not be able to see what is next for Summerwind, a bigger shame you have yet to see what happens to our son."

"Why! Why are you—"

The door closes in as Celacine, Elliot's mom and queen of Slimhixe, gets enclosed in the horse drawn wagon by two of her own guards.

"Take her to Shadowfalls." The king wipes some of the snot from his nose and takes a swig from a goblet one of his guards is holding. "When they find the body, we will tell them it was nothing but the wilderness."

"And your son, my king?" the goblet-bearing guard chimes in.

"Ah!" He chants out with his arms. "Nearly forgot about why I was here! Yes, yes, bring me to the boy!"

I follow along with the goblet-bearing guards, his three friends, and the king as they make their way through the camp, finding myself against the crackly wall and nearing the other side before they walk into a tent in front of me. The curtains expand, and I see Elliot strung up by his hands with blood pouring from his chest down to his toes.

"Ah! Elliot! My boy!" The king walks up and presses his hands against his cheeks. Eli squirms around while trying to spit out the gag in his mouth. The king shoves his hand inside his mouth and pulls it out in one fell swoop. "What say you?"

Elliot lets out a few coughs, some blood, some saliva, before finally lifting his head to the king's gaze.

"Fuck you!" He snarls. "You're such a fucking—"

The king delivers one blow to the gut and another quick one upwards into the bottom of his mouth.

"Oh, Elliot!" He laughs. "You have always been such a fucking disappointment. When they finally kill you, I will go back home and weep snake tears for your death."

"Go to the gates of hell." Eli coughs up some more phlegm.

"Maybe, once I am done my mourning, I will find comfort in a new queen and a new son that won't be such a fucking disappointment."

"The only thing you will—"

The king shoves his hand in Elliott's mouth and re-ties the gag behind his head as Elliott screams, then he picks up a new black rag and wraps it around Elliot's eyes so he cannot see anymore. Another punch to his son's head and another swift one to his gut.

"Goodbye...son." The king turns and makes his way out. The three guards follow suit, but the cupbearer is stopped by the king's arm against his chest. "Finish him."

The cupbearer nods his head and hands the goblet to another as the king and the remaining guards finally leave. The tent's curtains close behind them as I wait for the king and his men to get out of sight before approaching it myself.

I tightly grasp my sword in one hand as I slowly approach, assuring the coast is clear before finally pushing my way through.

The cupbearer turns to me while holding a knife, lunging immediately at my gut. A quick spin and slice and his arm detaches from his body. Blood squirts out from the base. A cowering scream rises as he falls onto his knees while clutching the stub. I spin once more and slice off his head.

I lift my sword up over my head and, with one slash, the rope holding Eli falls. I toss the blade to the side, catching him as he comes down before removing the gag from his mouth and then the blindfold from his eyes.

"Fuck you!" he yells while kicking and trying his best to punch. "Fuck you, fuck you!"

"Elliot!" I yell, grabbing his hands and bringing him into a hug. "It's me, it's me. I got you."

He ceases the attacks, and he brings his bloodied arms up around my neck for a hug.

"The king—" He sniffles and coughs.

I bring him away from my face to stare at him and place a hand over his cheek.

"It's okay, Little Fox." I draw him in for a hug. "I got you, son. I am not going anywhere."

I can only hope that she found peace. That the blood mage had done all she could.

Forever flying, that little bird. Forever in pain, that little girl.

Be free young firebird.

Be free.

-Elkhazen Valryn from his memoir, 'a bad f***king plan'

21

FATHERHOOD

We walk out of the camp.

"Do you have a horse?"

"Ahexnal," I whisper, waiting a few seconds until the mare gallops in front of us from seemingly nowhere.

"Is that an . . .?"

"Yup."

"Where did you get a—"

"Do not worry, let's get a move on."

Back on the horse, we travel south towards Shadowfalls.

"How long has my mother not been there?" Eli breaks the silence of the white noise.

"Not long, Little Fox. She only just got sent out mere moments before I got you down."

I stop the horse for a moment and hop down, helping Elliot down with my hand and taking a look at him.

"Why are we stopping?" he asks.

"Are you okay?" I kneel down to him and check to make sure his sword is sheathed properly to his belt and that he isn't bleeding as much from his mouth and nose onto his clothing.

"I will be." He tries to smile but it fades away within an instant. "Once we find my mother."

"Drink some more water," I say, passing him the waterskin on the side of the horse.

"Why don't we just keep going?" he asks, drinking a little bit, gargling some water, and spitting out blood.

"I need to make sure you are okay, first."

"I am."

"Look, Elliot." I place a hand on his shoulder. "I have been in your position. That feeling of being scared to save someone, your mind racing just as fast as your heart. When we find her, we will probably have to fight."

"Good!"

I rub my fingers over my eyes. "No, Eli...I have fought angry before. The largest scar on my back is from that one time. Not a lot of people get as lucky as I do, though. Most emotions overcome them in a fight, and they can barely hold a sword due to their shaking hands."

"So what do you want me to do, Vest?"

"I want you to make sure you are okay. The moment you get back on that horse, you save all of those thoughts of despair and fear for once your mother is safe, okay?" I bring my palm through his hair, messing it up a little before jumping back on the horse. "Whenever you are ready, son."

Elliot does take a moment. Deep breaths, a slight twitch of his body, a grasp on the hilt of his blade before shaking his head a few times and looking up at me and lifting up a hand to be helped up onto the mare.

He looks determined. "Ready, Vesten."

"I know."

* * *

Trying to keep our pace up while heading south feels as tedious as this entire journey has been. I fear what will continue to happen the longer I am away from home.

Off in the distance, seeing the same carriage that originally picked up the prince's mother and queen of Slimhixe feels like a sigh of relief.

It means they have not yet reached their destination, they have not yet exiled his mother, and they have not yet killed her.

"Get ready, Elliot," I call out behind me as I fling the reins down and make the horse go faster.

I reach behind my back and swing out *Erron*. I swing it around with my right hand while the left steers just to the side of the wagon. One guard at the front steers their carriage while the back is only big enough for one to two maximum. I wait for my sword to grow bright orange before galloping in front of the large horse that sits at the front.

Flinging myself off the still-moving horse, I plunge my sword's glowing steel into the snow and dirt. The orange disappears with a sizzle in the snow as bright blue and purple lightning bolts shoot out from the metal, hitting a few things all around and terrifying the horse enough to halt its travel toward the lights.

The guard controlling the reins flies off with the horse's sudden movement, and, for a brief moment, the wagon's front wheels rise into the air before falling down with a thud.

The guard that has just flown off the front of the carriage falls in front of me and whimpers at the ground. His arm is twisted at a strange angle, and it hangs limp.

"Elliot." I hear him run up behind me with his blade drawn. "He's yours."

I walk away from the guard as he stares up at the young man holding a small steel blade.

"Wait! Wait!" He coughs, holding his arm. "We were just following orders."

"That's my fucking mom, man." Elliot stabs the blade into him and twists before bringing it out and running up beside me.

"Alright, Little Fox. Put your ear up to the wood and tell me how much you hear."

He nods his head and gently places his ear over the cold wood, flinching for just a moment before lifting up one finger. I nod at him to open it and sheathe my sword to the scabbard on my back.

The door swings open and a guard walks out holding an axe. He stares at me confused for a moment as I rub my hands between each other to keep them warm.

"Hey, man!" I say as Elliot hides behind the door. "I am here to relieve you."

"Didn't get no orders about a new post?" He spits on the ground.

"Oh, fuck, my bad. I worded that terribly…I meant to say the prince will relieve you of your life."

Elliot walks out and tries his best to mimic a move of mine. He pirouettes in place perfectly before slashing away at the back of the guard, piercing the armour so they fall down like a thrown away toy. All while hobbling on his damaged leg.

"Elliot?" comes a voice from behind Eli as he turns to see his mother. She has the same dark hair as him and wears very typical high end fur robes for the cold.

She hobbles her way out and nearly falls in the snow before I catch her.

"You okay, Ma'am?" I ask, double-checking to see she is not bleeding or sustaining any life-threatening injuries.

"Absolutely," she snarkily replies, much like Elliot sometimes does. "It will take a lot more than a few punches to take down a queen."

"Mom!" Elliot hobbles over and hugs her. The sword still in one hand and dangling awfully close to her head, I carefully remove it and sheathe it for him, so he doesn't accidentally stab his mother after saving her. "This is Vesten!"

"Vesten, I see you taught my son how to use a sword."

"Whatever keeps the true heir safe, ma'am."

"Don't do that," she says.

"What?" I respond.

"Act like you care about royalty. I grew up with men who grew up in pig shit with better lying." She scoffs. "Royalty wouldn't teach a boy to use a sword or find himself all the way out here to save a queen…so why are you doing it?"

"I…uhh." I look down at Elliot, who shrugs his shoulders unknowingly. "I am the boy's protector."

"No shit, Vesten," she quips.

"Well—"

"Good." She takes a deep breath. "Fucking gates of hell, *someone had too.*"

I blink a few times into the void, completely unaware of how I thought this interaction was going to go.

"Do you know how to get to Klikia?" I ask her. She nods her head. "Brilliant, travel there and look for any ship heading to Aestas. Keep your true family tree down and they won't even question you being there."

"Thank you, Vesten. Be a dear and hand me that axe."

I reach down and lift up the dead guard's axe, giving it to her. She kinda reminds me of my wife.

"So about the king—" I ask.

"Kill the bastard." She spits onto the ground.

"You won't mind?" Elliot now asks.

"Oh, sweet thing. Your father used to be a good man, used to only care for you and me. Now he cares for the drink, sex, and fortune of war. He is not the same man, and the sooner we send him to Lwo…the better for everyone."

Celacine walks over to the carriage and towards the large horse. Cutting the reign with her new axe and patting the long snout of the horse, she returns to Elliot and brings him in for a big hug.

"I'll send a raven once everything is settled." He laughs gleefully. "Be safe, please."

"Usually, I would say be safe." She looks up at me. "But it seems you two have been keeping rather well for yourselves considering you're against an entire kingdom. I am sure the guards will have an herb treatment for your leg, Elliot."

"Safe travels," I say. "I'll find the treatment for the boy. When the matter with the king is solved, Elliot and I will come back for you. Stay low and stay safe."

She nods her head and turns back to the now-unlocked horse.

"You are more a protector to that boy than his true blood ever will be, Vesten. Don't forget that."

22

REMORSE & ALL IT BRINGS

Back on the road with just the two of us, everything feels right despite the new bruises. Once Celacine has made her way, we both head up through Slimhixe to Remorse where we plan on killing the king. *Huh, kinda odd to think about.*

"How did you find me anyway?" Elliot winces, rubbing away at his leg with the treatment still stinging his skin. He will be fine, but he may have a slight hobble or feel pain if he puts too much weight on his leg.

"Interrogated one of the dudes that captured me."

"You know, at this point, you would think I am just kinda used to you getting out of impossible scenarios, but every time you say something new, it impresses me." He laughs.

"Actually, for this one I had otherworldly help."

"What do you mean?"

"Well, this is gonna sound odd." I laugh. "Basically there were these cryptic trials I had to do in the afterlife."

"Lwo?"

"No...The Keeper actually."

"It's all real?"

"Yeah...yeah I guess so," I smile. "My father actually knew this keeper. Took on the shape of a young bird."

"So cool," Elliot says.

"Very."

"So does that mean The Keeper brought you back for a reason?" He sounds excited.

"I mean...originally that's what I thought. However, if that were the case, why would she make me do all of the trials?"

"Well, what were the trials?" He tries to hide his eagerness to learn more.

"The first was me on an island with my son," I say.

"The one that has yet to be born?"

"No, Erron. The one with a quirk."

"Oh...sorry."

"Everything felt real, the heat from the orbs shining upon us. The moment I started questioning the reality of it, though...the quicker everything turned sinister. Apparitions of him appearing, trying to kill me, and blaming me for his death."

"Keepers breath, Vesten!" He sounds just as shocked, as if he was there. "How did you do it?"

"I just kept reminding myself it was all in my head. The trials were my biggest fears, and I knew that."

"What was the final one like?"

"The last one was with Amarille in our home with baby Erron. The day just kept resetting over and over until I finally jumped out the front door to come back to reality."

"That sounds super confusing, Vesten."

"I suppose it's easier to explain if it ever happens to you." I laugh.

"You will see her soon, your wife," he says cheerfully. "We are nearing the end of the line, and that means soon you will be on a ship towards Aestas."

I debate telling him about the red rain proclamation that fills my mind, what all of this could mean, and why I was granted this fate, how I came back from the gates with a message and a horse for the seemingly simple job of saving the prince.

• • •

"Are you sure you wanna go through with this? I know your father is a bad man, but if anyone ever finds out—"

"Don't bother trying to be all serious and stuff, Vesten. I know what we are doing is right, and that's all that matters. Once the king is dead, I will take his place, and then everything will finally be different."

"When I first started mercenary work, I worked for Slimhixe. Most of the things I would do would be typical protection or travel and transport. One day, however, I found myself in a small town north of Remorse where there had been a distress call from a father. I opened the door, and a father had killed his daughter after finding out she had a quirk. At first no one realized why, until they found the mother in the back burned alive due to the daughter."

"That's horrifying."

"I still think about that man a lot, what must have gone through his own head before killing his own blood. What went through the daughter's head who no doubt hid away her quirk until it became too much to control. I just don't know how someone can do it, kill someone they love and not go insane."

"I don't love him though, Vest." I hear a sniffle from him behind me on the horse. "How can I, right? After everything he has done to me? My mother?"

* * *

The horse finally pulls up to the front of Remorse. Now in the middle of the night and approaching the morning, I want nothing less than to sleep away the past few nights' troubles. I'm excited as all hells to find myself back in a warm bed and not strung up from the ceiling in a place with an active fireplace.

There does not seem to be many people here compared to before. I wonder if most of them were only visiting for a brief time or if we've chosen a time to visit that is not as busy. After all, it's the middle of the night.

We leave the horse out front on a wooden post next to some water and food. The soon-to-be king and I walk into the same tavern we visited before. The "Remorse-full-Drink" has not changed much since our last visit. There is still a large Orcish man and a few others walking around and serving drinks. We pick the same table in the corner away from everyone as we did a few days ago.

A new server we haven't seen before with bright blonde hair walks over and pours out a goblet of alcohol for Elliot and me. He and I both happily accept and down the beverages, which at this point feels like a luxury. The past few days of being tortured and on the verge of death makes this alcohol taste as sweet as any Summerwind fruit.

Within a few moments, the man who just served us is pouring some more of the drink, opting to just leave the jug with us and nod his head to go serve some other patrons and not be stuck in this corner all night.

"Fuck me, this alcohol is good." Elliot laughs.

"Agreed, Little Fox."

"So, that's new." He giggles while sipping a little less intensely. "The nickname, I mean."

"Yeah—" I place the cup down. "I—used to call Erron that."

"Oh."

"Sorry, Eli, I know that's a big jump from—"

"I like it." He wastes no time responding.

"Oh, really?" I take a sip.

"The first few days to however many weeks we've known each other, you called me boy, so yes, I will gladly take this new title."

"I trust you, Eli," I say. "Like a son."

"And I trust you too, like a father. But if you and I have to keep saying it out loud to one another so it feels real, maybe that's a bit excessive."

"Agreed," I say. "I never much liked showing too many emotions."

He smiles. "I know, Vesten. Sort of pieced that together myself."

The door opens and a panting patron enters. Someone wearing typical rags but drenched in sweat from his forehead down to his shoes that look like he's been running in water. Some patrons take notice of the panting man, but Eli and I opt to avoid him, drinking another sip from our approaching-empty beverages.

"Vesten Autumnspark!" he cries out while searching through his slanted over shoulder bag. "Frohv?"

Eli and I look up from our cups and glance at one another before walking over to the man at the front of the bar.

"Billy!" I cry out with a fake name.

"Billy, you silly drunkard!" Elliot joins in as we both push him out of the tavern.

"Come here, ya drunk! Clearly you have had too much!" I call out to any passerby before we throw him in between the tavern and the building to the side of it.

I kick out the front of his foot so he falls directly into the cold blanket of snow beneath himself.

"What are y—"

A swift punch across his face and even Elliot lays in for a few hits before he crawls back to the other end of the homes. One hand on the hilt of my sword, I walk steadily closer to him before he raises a hand in anticipation.

"Amarille sent me!" he screams just before he is about to hear the hiss of my sword.

"What?" I bring the sword back fully into its sheath.

"I am from Aestas! I bring the word!"

"Fucking gods, man!" I reach over and help him up. "Next time, damn, open with that before yelling my name in this town. This time last week there were wanted posters of me, and I do not think people forget that easily."

"Apologies." He holds the bottom part of his tunic to cover the blood leaking from his nose. "It's about your son, he was born in the night a few days ago."

"What!" I excitedly scream as I bring him into a big hug. Some of his blood smears on my gambeson. "Amarille, she is okay then?"

"She and the baby are perfectly healthy, Froh'v. Named it after yourself, Vesten the 3rd!"

"Brilliant!" I turn and look down towards Elliot who smiles up at me. "Thank you, sir! For delivering—"

"There is more," the messenger says, now looking rather distressed. "Your father...he passed around the same time."

The tone of the situation abruptly switches with the disappearance of my smile. Tears well in my eyes before a few fall and hit the snow beneath me.

"Fuck," I whisper.

"Sorry, Froh'v."

"Amara." I look up towards him. "She didn't have the baby alone, did she?"

"She did."

"Fuck!" I turn my body to the wooden wall of the tavern and slam my fist into it. The wall does not break but, instead, I hear a crack in the fingers at the top of my right hand. I slightly shake my hand now as I lift one finger, which is bleeding from the knuckle into my palm.

"Deliver her the message. I will be back in no later than a week, aye?"

"Aye, Froh'v. Sorry about—"

"Now!" I yell at the poor messenger before he nods his head and hurries off, still clutching his bloody nose.

"Vesten, I am sorry." Elliot reaches over and grabs my bloodied hand.

"He was a good man, better than I."

"You—"

"So, let's just leave it at that for now, aye?" I turn and attempt to give a smile in his direction. "We have a job to do…let's go get another drink."

I think Elliot has gotten better at realizing when I do not want to talk. Opting to instead just smile at me and nod his head, he takes my arm and leads me back inside the tavern. This time we enter the establishment and see most of it has cleared out except for a few girls and guys in the corner awaiting pay for pleasure. In the large centre table, I see a familiar face.

"Supplying enemy troops now?" I walk over and take a seat across from Diania who looks up surprised.

"Fucking up my sword now?" She smiles while chugging down some unknown brown alcohol. Elliot sits down at the chair beside me.

"I see you two are still going strong. How odd."

"Travelling across the world will do that to people."

"Vest." Elliot taps my shoulder. "I am going to go to sleep. Can I have some coins?"

I laugh and reach into my coin purse, giving him just enough for the room. "Actually, I was hoping for a bit more."

He looks at me and then behind him towards the people standing around waiting for someone to buy their company for the night. I catch the attention of one of the girls staring over at me and motion her over.

"Here," I say while I hand the dark-haired girl a few coins. "Be safe."

Elliot nearly jumps out of his seat, ushering a thank you before linking arms with the woman and walking towards the rooms.

"He has taken a liking to you." Diania chuckles.

"He is better than most of the people on this gods forsaken continent. Sometimes I forget Slimhixe is where he was born."

"You know, a good father probably would not buy his new son a person's company for the night."

"Yeah, well." I reach over the table and pick up her goblet. "Been a long week for the two of us."

"I can tell." She reaches over and takes her goblet back. "I was supposed to deliver a new sword to a captain out near Boneshiver. Doubt you would know anything about that, would you?"

"Just that I doubt he will be needing it," I say, almost flinching at the pain affiliated with the name. "Actually, if it's all the same I think Eli could use a new blade."

"Not gonna do me any good anymore." She looks down into her cup and then back at me like she is biting her tongue. "This thing you're doing with the prince." She lowers her voice slightly. "Be careful, Vesten. Even back in Klikia you were always someone who didn't think before drawing a blade."

"No blades have been drawn excessively. He is a good kid."

"And being good is what gets people killed in this world. What is stopping him from killing you after killing the king?"

"How do you know we plan—"

"I am old, not dull. My mind is sharp as your sword and can cut you apart like cake."

"Why would he do that?" I scoff quickly at the thought.

"No more loose ends, Vesten."

"Fuck you." I slam my fist down onto the table. "How dare you even inquire about such a thing!"

She widens her eyes and flinches, taking a step back and realizing the error of her phrasing. "I am sorry, Vest. You know I do not mean to compromise our friendship."

I look down at the table at the blood from my hand seeping into the wood. "Sorry, it's been a long week."

The Orc man walks over and passes me a goblet. Noticing the blood seeping into the table, he sighs before pulling out a white rag from behind himself and throwing it over my hand.

"Clean it up," he coarsely says as he walks back to the bar.

"So . . ." I try to break the awkward tension between Diania and me. "I suppose this means we are even?"

She loudly cackles and spits some drink out of her mouth. "If that boy is to become king? I think not! You AND he owe me immensely now."

I laugh as well before lifting myself out of the chair and nodding my head at her.

"With love, Vesten the 2nd."

"With love, Diania…the hag." I wink at her.

"Don't make me regret giving you this." She reaches under the table and pulls out a sword covered in black cloth.

I take it from her and curtsy, no doubt pissing her off at the formality. Not everyone has to act like the mercenaries and smugglers of Klikia all the time. That can be exhausting.

I walk through the tavern and pass the Orcish man who grits his tusks and points me in the direction of the prince. I approach the door and give a few swift knocks to no answer, then open it with a twist of the wrist and walk in.

The two girls he had sent to his room still wear their clothes and, instead, just simply scratch the top of his head as he sleeps. He does indeed look rather cozy, but that was not what I expected him wanting to pay two women for their services for.

"Did he?" I whisper.

"No m'lord, he actually passed out before doing anything of note."

"Huh."

I open the door with one hand and expose the opening so the two know that they must leave now. Both humbly agree and smile back at the snoring boy before I close the door and steal one of the many pillows the prince has stolen for himself. Placing it gently on the ground, I remove the belt that holds my pouches and blade.

Taking a few deep breaths, I stare wide-eyed at the ceiling, knowing what tomorrow will hold for us both, how our actions could impact the history of Verenden forever. Despite all of the important actions I have found myself on, one thing since the start that has remained the same: I am ever so excited to finally see my wife and child.

23

A FUCKING SHIT PLAN

I wake up to the sound of the door opening and shutting rather abruptly. There's swift movement and my blade is drawn with the tip facing the door where I see Elliot standing in the doorway confused as all hells.

I look out the window and see the orbs have barely even picked their way out of the skies.

"Sorry," he says, clearly nervous.

"Where did you run off to? It's early," I say.

"Had to get some fresh air, that's all."

There's a slight stutter to his voice. His eyes look away from me as he speaks about his whereabouts, and his hands are crossed over one another. Maybe it's just because I used to have a rather reckless son whom I had to keep an eye on to avoid fires being started, but I know when someone is lying.

"Aye." I stand up and put on my belt. "I suppose since we are both up, we know we should be on our way to Triumpth."

"Yeah…let's go." He turns almost immediately to make haste for the door.

"Elliot." I stand up and stare into his worried eyes. "I got something for you."

I reach underneath the bed and pull out the black-clothed sword. Walking over to him, I place it in his open arms with a quick reveal of the beautiful blade, its cross guard matching the one on my sword. Jewels run all throughout it, inscribed horses galloping in the metal. It looks rather similar to my sword except without the tip slightly forged in one direction, and I imagine when he spins it, it will not emit lighting of any kind.

"It's beautiful, thank you."

I do not know what I'm about to say next, only that he's walked out of the room too quickly for me to say anything, swiftly making his way down the stairs and out of the tavern. I nearly have to run to keep up with his increased pace. Getting to the horse, I attempt to jump on but have no luck.

"Elliot, hold on." I run over to him outside. "What's going on?"

"It's nothing, Vest."

"I have been married long enough to know that 'it's nothing' usually means it's something."

He doesn't smile or respond. He just stares at the ground and kicks some of the snow with his boot. "Elliot, you gotta let me in here."

"It's just…after today, that's the end."

"The end of what?"

"This, us, everything."

"Eli." I lift up his chin to meet my gaze. "Aye, this journey will come to an end, but that does not mean we will part ways."

"I will be king. That means I will not be able to come to Aestas. We will never see each other again."

"Aye, you will be king. You also will still be my son." I smile at him. "Elliot, even if the two of us are apart, we are still family."

"Will you come visit?" He finally meets my gaze.

"I mean if you send a ship, sure."

He hits me on my shoulder.

"Not funny," he says snarkily.

"I know, Little Fox. But you and I have a job to do, aye?"

"Aye." He tries to mimic my accent but sounds like a broken songbird.

A smile back up at me is all that's needed before I say Ahexnal, and

I help him up onto the back of the horse. Elliot takes his old blade and throws it aside to sheathe his new one across his belt.

* * *

OFF AND AWAY TOWARDS TRIUMPTH. Everything feels dead this far north. There are no more sights and spectacles, only ruined land where battles took place and a grey overtone. Even the islands Of Verenden had more to offer than this contrasting dullness, made even more repulsive by the cold wind hitting my face.

I know I have to remain focused and not get distracted, but I can still feel myself warm up at the thought of soon seeing Amarille. Gods help me, she will probably be pissed at me for a few things, but I just miss being around her.

Passing by a few of the wagons on the trail down to Remorse, I realize we should probably have a good story for getting in. I do not imagine the capitol of Slimhixe will be so kind to strangers that do not have much to offer.

"So what is the game plan once we get there?" I ask Elliot.

"The guards should recognize me and let us straight in."

"Won't they care about the bounty?" I laugh. Surely Slimhixe men can't be that dull?

"There is this old passageway that leads underneath the city and directly into the kingdom. Supposed to be used for emergencies."

"That's our way in?" I ask.

"By the time we have entered, it will be too late to stop us...which means that once we arrive later today, it should be the perfect time to go in and kill him."

"Diabolical." I laugh. "Especially from you."

"Just doing what is best for my people."

"Spoken like a true king."

"Shut up."

In the cold snowfall and utter gray landscape, finally, off in the distance, we see something of note: Triumpth itself.

Tall thick metal walls covering all sides with one entrance in the front look more like a dog kennel than the town in which the king resides. I can understand the need to protect the citizens and social life in order to win wars, but I doubt much of the orbs' light even seeps its way into the town. Only for a few moments of the day when the orbs are just above would everyone get some light.

It's massive, the walls stretching from one end to another, protecting even the simple farm folk deep in those thick walls. I wonder if there are any issues of anyone attempting to climb and falling to their death from the easily one-hundred foot or higher metal wall. It makes it impossible to see inside aside from the small fractions of civilization visible through the entryway.

Triumpth, however, is known for something that to this day has started a debate on their true feelings of magic. Green magic spurts from the ground and hovering pieces of land in the air are only possible to climb from elevators at the base that are controlled by one person spinning a wheel.

Of course, the source of the magic required to lift small bits of land that hoist giant crossbows are now down to urban legends. Slimhixe seems to be the only place that ever controlled this power effectively. The only other that comes close is the smaller floating civilization of Imperium on the islands Of Verenden.

Floating crossbows that can monitor 360 degrees and large metal walls mean Triumpth is an impregnable base. Not to mention, we haven't even gotten to the castle's own walls yet. I used to see those giant ballistas on Man O'War ships and would wave to them while sailing, always telling myself, one day, I would become high ranking enough to have my own.

Elliot and I approach closer and closer on the trail towards the base. The walls only seem to get larger and larger until they cast a large shadow over us. Every guard in Slimhixe is a frozen horse, twenty of them outside the front gate with two on each side to assure no one tries anything suspicious.

"Alright, Eli." I stretch my back and put on my fake smile. "Best hope your plan works."

"It will, Vesten."

I casually bring the horse's reins into both hands and bring myself just in front of the ten guards.

"Halt!"

"Halt!"

Ten or so of the men and women in front of us lift up their varying weapon types.

"What is your business here?" a coarsely voiced male on the right side says. I try to identify the source but, due to them wearing matching horse-shaped helmets, it's hard to tell.

Elliot leans over and jumps off the horse as gracefully as he can. Nothing happens for a few moments as he awkwardly stares down the men and women. I join him on the ground.

"Wait a minute?" One of the closer voices on the left side says, and

I place one hand over my sword. "He's the prince!"

"Open the gate!"

"The prince is back!"

The fake smile comes back on as one of the guards rushes over and grabs the reins from my hand, patting the back of my shoulder as we are escorted inside.

"How were your travels, prince?" a significantly younger voice asks from one of the five people following us inside the raised gate.

"Well, very well."

"I thought you were kidnapped?" He sounds rather unprofessional.

"I was in Klikia, then this man here saved me," he says.

A few of the horse-shaped helmets turn to face my direction and then immediately go back to the prince.

"Shall we alert the king of your arrival?" one of the female guards asks.

"Unnecessary." He smiles at me. "We actually came to surprise him."

"Brilliant!"

"Amazing idea, prince!"

"Shall we, Froh'v?" Elliot asks me before he and I make our way through the gate.

I walk up beside him and meet him there. Together walking into Triumpth, the first thing I realize is we are barely fucking there. Farm fields are everywhere, nothing but typical farm fields with fireballs floating above them to keep the crops warm this far north.

In front of us, I can see a large hilltop castle off in the distance with its own bloody set of tall metal walls like the outskirts, covered in gold and reflecting just as much from the orbs as the walls.

Just before that, there's the city which seems to be thriving with civilization. It feels odd to see what is, essentially, an entire province of resources hidden behind these walls. The dull gray of everything leading to here has now disappeared. Green lights reflect from the floating crossbow islands where a few men all sit around on giant ballistas waiting to fire at someone. I have only ever seen a few of them on large Slimhixe royal Man O'War ships. The ones everyone smart tries to avoid.

"I like to imagine the ballistas were used for dragons back when they were ever so prevalent in Verenden," Elliot says, smiling. "Mother used to tell me stories about back when they used to be everywhere."

"A few thousand years ago," I chuckle. "Must have been quite a sight."

"Funny," Elliot chuckles. "Funny that Slimhixe is so anti-magic yet we have floating islands strictly for ballistas."

"Wait." I stop walking and look down at him. "Even you do not know the source of it?"

"Not even the king does."

"Weird."

The orbs now leaving the sky have left us in the dark earlier than expected. The tall walls mean that the orbs leave the sight of everything a lot faster and leave everything feeling extra cold and extra dark. It would be impossible to see if not for the fireballs floating around the crops.

"Where is the entrance?" I ask Elliot.

"Follow me." He takes my hand. "It's just before reaching the city portion."

I look around at the farmers as we walk through, their faces barely ignited by the fireballs that float around. I check for scars on their faces or visible parts of their bodies marked from the empire's doing. Sadly, in the darkness it's hard to make out.

One goblin tending the fields has their face burned halfway down the side. I wonder if the empire will force that man to tell them it was a simple accident with the fireball. I wonder if the empire just thinks no one knows what happens to the farmers who do not work as hard. Of course, I would not know any of this if I did not switch my allegiance and learn first-hand from people.

Most of the men and women on my ship were people that hated Slimhixe. Most of them are also farmers and have more scars than I have.

Just before reaching the entrance of the city, Elliot veers us right and towards a large farm building surrounded by guards and cattle. There are only about four guards this time, rather conservative resources for Slimhixe. Each of them simply stands guard, two on each side of the large red barn doors.

"Gentlemen and Gentlewomen." Elliot once again takes the lead. "Looking to get into the castle through the passage."

"The king did not give us any attention to this matter," one of the female guards says through the hallowed mask.

"It is a surprise. Merian knows about it." He scowls at the lot of them. "Unless you want me to contact him directly, I demand you let me and my acquaintance in."

"Apologies, M'lord."

Elliot quickly takes my hand and leads me into the barn. There are a few horses around, some cows, and other various animals I cannot recognize at the moment. The barn, however, is completely empty. Nothing along the walls or even anything on the floor, the only thing being a small wooden door on the floor in the centre.

"How many people know about this?" I ask.

"Just the guards stationed and high-ranking royalty."

"Think anyone else will be in the tunnel?"

"Gods no. I used to come down to it to think. No one ever goes down the tunnels."

Elliot grabs my hand and leads me to the opening the hatch, then flings it open to reveal a concrete tunnel around all sides. I jump down first, making sure everything around us is all secure. There doesn't seem to be anyone else down here, but something still feels amiss.

I bring my hand down and press my palm against the floor, feeling slight vibrations.

"Eli." I stop moving.

"Yes, Vesten?"

"Something doesn't make sense, Little Fox."

"What do you mean?" He looks confused, approaching and standing in front of me.

"Your father wanted you dead, the guards let you in twice with open arms, and now…there are no guards here?" I cross my arms.

"Well, of course the guards around here do not know anything."

"But that's what doesn't make sense." I notice now the slight shake in his hand and my eyes go wide. "If the guards do not know, how come they are running to our position as we speak?"

"I don't know what you m—" Elliot kicks the lower part of my shin.

I fall down to the ground, and he draws his new sword and places it against the bottom part of my throat.

"Oh, Little Fox, why?" I feel the slight crack in my voice.

The footsteps get gradually louder with Elliot's shaking hands. A part of me debates trying to steal the sword from him, using him as leverage to escape, but he probably thought that through as well. I was outplayed by him for once, believing that I was something to him the same way he was to me.

The multiple frozen horses run in and take over, pointing their various weapons at my neck. I still look into Elliot's eyes, noticing the trembling of his legs and throat as sweat pours off his forehead.

"Take him away," he says.

I dare not take my eyes off Eli as the guards forcefully pull my hands away from me and slam my face to the cold concrete ground. Elliot walks over and steals the sword from my scabbard.

"Oh, Little Fox…I truly did underestimate you."

One of the guards stands over me, slamming her metal boot down onto my face. A swift thud, and everything goes black.

24

LIKE FATHER LIKE SON

The first thing I notice when I wake is a stinging pain on my wrist. Where am I? How long have I been here? Where is Eli?

My vision comes back to me in blips of black cloudy vision until I finally see the metal guard standing in front of me. Two more behind me breathe heavily down my neck as I hang in the air tied to a rope from the ceiling.

I wiggle my toes to make sure they still work and move both my fingers as well. One set of fingers presses against the rope that holds me in the air, the other against metal armour. A slight stinging sensation fills my right wrist as I shake it but feel the strength of someone pressing against it to keep it in place.

It takes a second for my mind to come back to me, for me to even remember the dire situation I've brought myself into.

I recognize the stinging. I look over to see someone holding an ink quill commonly used for tattoos. My vision is still hazy. I barely see past the rows of armour in front of my face before catching a glimpse of what they are working on. A blood quirk tattoo.

I shake my wrist and fling my body around but feel nothing helps. My wrist gets slight levity but that is because it is the only thing not strapped tightly to the ceiling. The rest of my body sways back and forth like a hung pig with a poor executioner.

"Fuck off of me," I snarl in a wheeze for breath and thirst for water.

"Shut up." The one tattooing my wrist chuckles. "You'll be burned early tomorrow morning, so no need to blabber on." Fuck.

Is this how I am to die? After everything that has happened. Strung up to a spire and burned alive like my first son. I suppose there's a sense of poetic nihilism in that. I suppose with Elliot truly turned against me, there's nothing I can do to stay the tides.

Even if I were given a sword and had to fight my way out, I would be outnumbered and deep inside the northern walls of an unbreathable and inescapable place known to all.

The door thuds open with the king's loud and obnoxious footsteps making it clear who's coming before I see his face enter the frame. His long, jagged black beard and lack of hair, multiple rings on both hands, and over-the-top, gaudy golden robe are more than what I want to take notice of him.

"A chip off the old block, isn't he?" the king says, Elliot now following behind him in more extravagant and gaudy robes himself. "A true slayer of beasts! A true slayer of women! Ahaha!"

If this guy keeps talking, I will throw myself onto the spire early.

"What's next for him?" Elliot does not even bother calling me by my name.

"He will burn atop the spire like all those other quirks who have come before him!" The king cackles.

"But—but he does not have a quirk?" Elliot now seems confused.

"Aye, he does not! But the people out there . . ." He reaches over and brings Elliot into a close embrace to the side of his large body. "The people out there will only see what we see."

"A person?"

"A monster."

I stare at Elliot, waiting for him to notice me and stare back, but when I look at him, I see nothing, just a blank canvas staring down towards the floor as his father rocks him from side to side.

The guard finishes tattooing my wrist. I try to move it away and squirm to be free before they tie my hand to the top but to no use. The guards surrounding me lift up my arm with ease and tie it into the other.

I just continue to dangle from the wooden ceiling of this castle. I look around and try to find where exactly I am. Dust resembling a bed underneath my feet, multiple torches, and nice wooden architecture mean this is probably the guest bedroom. I wonder why they do not just throw me into the dungeon. My eyes continue to gaze around the room until the feeling of black ink rolls down my arm and down to my stomach.

A bird flying and dripping blood is now forever inked into my wrist. Something so simple as a design that is just as easy to acquire as any other tattoo, yet it is the reason why most people live their lives in fear. The fire quirk tattoo is the reason my son has already met the same fate I am awaiting.

"Leave us." The king raises his arms, and they all disperse immediately. Elliot stays close to him. "Also, one of you bring the sword."

What sword? The question quickly answers itself when one of the silver-plated guards walks over to him holding an unsheathed blade, my blade.

"Put that down!" I yell.

The king, unfazed, comes over to meet my swinging body. "Or what?"

He places the side of the blade across my chest, gently pushing his hand inward until the sharp steel pierces through some skin and blood seeps into it. He finishes his diagonal cut quickly as I let out a cry of pain. The blade glows more and more orange as he waves it across the room like a fireball in a field.

"Never actually used one of these," the king snarls. "Does this one light on fire like others?"

"No," Elliot answers for me.

"Curious to see what it does then."

He completes his frantic and unskilled waving of the sword around the room. The blade glows bright orange, and his smile grows wider. "Sure hope this does not kill you then."

He raises it high up in the air, and I close my eyes. I know the blade is at full charge, and I know that the moment it touches my skin, it will kill me without even letting me have a final say.

"Wait," Elliot chimes in, and I open my eyes to see the sword a few inches from my chest. "I wanna do it."

"Aha!" the king chants. "Brilliant! Like father, like son!"

The king, very unsafely, nearly drops the blade into Elliot's hands. Eli now chooses to look me in the eyes and stare at me head on, a slight quiver of his lower lips, hands shaking as the blade walks back and forth in the air above my head. The king patiently stands behind him with his arms crossed.

Elliot turns his body, facing the king now with the tip of the sword.

"On your knees!" Eli yells.

"What are you doing you fucking—" the king tries to speak before Elliot kicks the lower part of his shin, and he falls to the ground. "Put down the blade, and listen to your father, *boy*."

"You are not my father." Elliot raises the blade high in the air. "The man tied up is."

With one quick crackling slash, the orange blade hits the king's neck. Purple bolts of lighting shoot across the room, burning some of the wooden floor. A quick slash, and the king is dead. No time for a final speech or monologue, no time for a final breath before his own blood ended his life.

"All my fucking life!" Elliot slams the blade back down into his chest, not cutting fully but still spurting out some blood. "All of my fucking life I wanted to impress you!" The blade once again glows orange.

"Elliot!" I try to make him stop.

"All my life I believed you fucking cared!" He brings the blade down once again. "I—am—not—your fucking son!"

"Little Fox!" I scream.

The blade once again disperses its electrical current into him, this time some of the bolts find their way to his head and explode the king's eyes like a cherry tomato. Elliot does a spin and slashes away at the top of the rope causing me to fall to the floor.

I hit the ground hard, but without the bound hands, I am able to lift myself up into a sitting position. I quickly wipe away the red hair in front of my face and use the back of my hand to wipe away my sweat.

Eli turns to me. "Sorry."

The door opens with an older gentleman in fine robes barging in. I use my hands to push myself in front of Elliot as the man looks around at the many burn marks and his own king dead on the floor.

"Went to plan, Elliot?"

"It did, Merian."

"I am sorry," Merian says, now revealing a small smile. "Let me rephrase that…went to plan, my king?"

"You did all of this on purpose?" I sit down on the floor as Elliot walks in front of me.

"While we were in Remorse, I sent a letter to my old steward and told him the plan." Elliot motions towards Merian. "I knew we would never be able to kill the king any other way. Not with the amount of guards he launders with himself."

"Aren't those the same guards that will kill you and me now?" I chuckle.

"No, idiot." He smiles at me. "I am their king."

"Gods be damned, Little Fox."

"I would never actually *let* them kill you. This was the only way that guarantees you live and, quite frankly, I am not done bossing you around yet," he says.

"I was scared." I finally drop my smile.

"Of what?" He walks over to me.

"That you didn't mean any of the words that you said."

"Well," he says, placing a hand on the top of my head and ruffling my hair like I do to him. "You are not as smart as me, clearly."

* * *

STANDING underneath the warm water of the shower in the king's room is something I never thought I'd do in my lifetime. Nor has it ever been something I ever considered possible. The boiling water washes away the dried blood from my body, and the newly sutured mark across my chest stings in the water.

Usually, when I shower, my mind takes me to the same few places it normally does involving Amara. Times when we escaped danger, times when we first kissed. Today, however, the water seems to bring back a different memory.

Me lying on her lap while trying to sleep. Her fingertips scratch the top of my scalp as she reads a book in the silence.

That was fucking nice.

I hear cheers from outside the open window of the room. On the other end of the corner where I stand underneath rushing water, I still end up hearing cheers somehow. I wonder if the crowd is pretending to be excited for their new king. I am sure for most of them, it does not affect their typical day who wears the crown. I am sure for most, however, that if they ever were to have a child with a quirk, they would not have to worry anymore.

My biggest question remains with Summerwind, wondering how they will react to not only the fact the previous king is dead, but that his son will now be removing the law against quirks. How the son of the king who burned people and children alike is now planning to ask the enemy to join banners.

"Sir." I hear the door open. "Sorry to disturb you but the king has requested your presence."

"Can the king's request wait until I have trousers on?" The door closes.

I stop the water from flowing and wipe my hands against my face before taking a deep breath. Walking to the bed, I see the orange robes that have been laid out for me to put on. Sighing, I fling them on, hating the itchy fabric of them. I'd much rather just continue to wear my bloody gambeson like always.

I walk over to the door and open it up to see Eli with one fist in the air like he was about to knock.

"I thought you requested me?" I look down at him and laugh.

"I didn't think you'd listen." He walks in and sits on the bed. "The crowd took it...well."

"I imagine it is going to take some getting used to," I say.

"Vesten." He breaks the silence as I sit down next to him. "There is a ship waiting for you at port."

"Eli." I chuckle and look down towards my bruised hands. "You were *just* crowned king, and it would be foolish of me to leave your side until you have more reliable protection."

"I am coming with you," he blatantly says.

"What about your kingdom?" I ask.

"They will need time to process the new laws and news of a potential alliance." He smiles at me. "It will be fine. I actually will be much safer on your new ship than I will be here for the moment."

"You nearly died on my ship last time." "Yeah…yeah, I almost did." We laugh.

"I can't wait for Amarille to meet you."

25

THE END OF SPRING

"How does the new ship feel?" The small king looks up at me as we walk around the main deck.

I will admit it does look awfully pretty. There is gold where wood would do just fine and tall sails with a fox head insignia. A full crew of people, some of whom even have their own quirks.

"Too perfect." I smile down at him and brush my hands through his hair to mess it up.

He moves away and readjusts his golden crown. "Gods, you are grumpy, aren't you?"

"Well, Little Fox, I think it is part of my charm."

"It's part of your something." Elliot laughs with me as we head up the stairs to the steering wheel. "Are you excited to finally travel home?"

"Well, honestly, I am scared shitless…my king."

"Fuck you." Elliot laughs at me. "Seriously, though, why are you afraid?"

"In the time I've been gone from my wife, I have lied to her about where I was going and who I was with, and I was not home for our child to be born into this world."

"Wait, you didn't even tell her about me?"

"I told her…." I cough, "of you…just left out some crucial parts."

"You did not tell her I am the King of Slimhixe, did you?"

"No."

I walk over to the side of the ship and place both my arms over the wood, staring down at the rushing water. Elliot walks over and does the same.

"You know," he says. "I think you may be overthinking this. She is your wife and, sure, you were not around cause you lied. And you didn't tell her you met the prince. And you weren't there for her child. And—"

"Does this lecture have a point?" I smirk down at him, appreciating what he is trying to do.

"She loves you." Elliot reaches over and puts his hand on mine. "A few lies can't change that."

"You know, I think you spending all this time around me is making you a better person."

"I doubt it," he quips back, nudging me with his shoulder and laughing.

"I miss her," I say, looking out at Aestas off in the distance. "A lot."

"I am excited to meet her since I can't imagine anyone thinking you would be a good significant other."

"I take back what I said about you being around me being good…I actually think it's making you much harsher." I turn to him and brush his hair once more before walking to the front of the ship.

Slowly we get closer and closer to Aestas and my home. Approaching, I am finally able to see it again. Smoke exudes from the top of it due to the large fireplace. I feel like I can already feel it on my skin. I am most looking forward to the smell of her hair. That may sound a bit off but, truly, it is one of the few things that make the home feel like a home…and I built the damned thing.

Closer and closer towards home, with each wave and gust of wind bringing me closer and closer, I forget how to breathe. My heart beats like it did on Amara's and my wedding day. Nervous for the future but excited to see her.

My child, the one who shares my name, is inside of that house, and I have yet to see him. I have yet to pick him up and teach him sea shanties while Amara tells me to knock it off. He will probably cry when he sees me, and I will probably do the same. While Amara and I were away from one another, she had a child, and I am coming back with the king, whom I consider to be my own blood.

If someone were to tell me a few months ago I would end up growing attached to the prince and now king of Slimhixe, I would probably tell them to fuck off.

The house is now closer than ever, and as the boat is about to dock, I quickly turn around and bring Elliot in for a big hug. He acts surprised at first but eventually realizes I am not going to stab him and hugs me back as tightly as he can. I lean down and kiss the top of his head, trying to avoid getting stabbed myself by the spiky crown.

"It's gonna be okay, Vesten." He giggles. "I have seen you fight off a horde of people and barely come out with a scratch…I am sure you can deal with a little marital dispute."

He's getting smarter, and I do not like it.

The tall wooden ramp lowers down onto the dock with a loud slam. The people of the crew act like not much has happened and instead just continue to perform their own individual tasks. The reason we even sailed this far away from Slimhixe and to Aestas is for no one other than myself.

Elliot joins me, and we walk down the ramp onto the snow. Walking along the cobblestone path leading upwards towards the home at the top of the hill, I feel like I can finally breathe again. My heart beats out of my chest, but that does not stop the large smile forming on my face from ear to ear.

The smile disappears when I notice something that was not there before. Just off to the side of everything, a small cobble headstone underneath the cover of a pine tree. Upon closer inspection, I see that it reads:

Vesten Autumspark
First Of His Name
Headmaster
Father

Husband

I REACH DOWN and feel the stone slab. Falling to my knees, I rub my thumb over his name.

"I am sorry, Vesten," Elliot says.

"He was a good man, better than I will ever be…I am just happy that now he is with Dennen. He deserved to be buried with him, but now all we can do is hope they have found one another."

"They have…they must've." Elliot places a hand on my shoulder, and I lift myself up.

"You're right." I smile down at him and, once again, scruff up his hair. "They must've. Now let's go check on Amara, aye?"

I take Elliot's hand and walk with him up the stairs and to the front door. One of my hands gently presses against it just to remember the feel. Thinking back to when I had met the Keeper, I remember how the feeling of this home felt slightly different in the dream than what it was supposed to.

One swift push of the wooden door, and I feel the warmth and smell of my home once again. The smell of balsam resin and the smoke from the crackling fire centrepiece in the middle of the room. The house still looks the same as when I left, cleaner even. No sign of Amarille, however.

"Amara!" I call out to the dismay of no one answering back.

Softly and faintly, I hear the sound of a baby crying directly in front of me, coming from inside my bedroom. Amarille would never leave our child alone for even a second, so something is amiss here.

I draw my sword from the scabbard along my back and hear the familiar hiss of the metal, swinging it around my side while Elliot does the same, holding his own blade up high. Arriving directly in front of the door, I lean down towards Eli.

"Wait here," I whisper. "And watch my back."

He nods his head, and I count down my fingers from three before kicking open the door and rushing in blade first, spinning my body around trying to find whether or not Amarille has been taken or injured. I study the wooden floors for any sign of blood, but nothing is there. Instead, at the front of the room, in front of the bed, I see a crib.

A crying infant sits in the crib while I take quick notice of its bright red hair.

"Vest!" I hear behind me, and I spin around holding my blade up high to see Amarille with her bow drawn at Elliot.

"What are you doing!" I yell out to Amara as she slowly walks forward in her fur tunic, still clutching an arrow tightly in place

Eli stands directly in between both of us. He slowly comes forward with discretion to the arrow pointed directly at his skull. Finally, all of us sit in the large bedroom with Elliot beside me and Amarille not releasing her arrow.

"Froh'v, you did it!" she cries out while smiling, a slight grit in her teeth as the bow lets out a tightening sound of the rope stressed in place. "You brought the king here!"

"Amarille, put the bow down," I try to plead with her. "He is not who you think he is."

"He is the king!" She snarls at me. "This is exactly what we needed, Vesten! Once he is dead, we will forever be able to live happily with our family!"

"Amara! Fucking put down the bow!" I try to yell while my sword radiates its orange aura. "He doesn't mean us any harm!"

She lowers her bow for a second before raising it back up with a bite of her tongue. "Do you have any idea how mad you sound? He is someone directly responsible for the death of Erron!"

"I didn't—"

Eli tries to get his two cents in, but Amara releases an arrow into his shoulder, causing his blade to fall and himself to tumble backwards. I run directly in front of him as he whimpers on the ground, lifting my arms to the side to protect him from any further arrows.

"Amara—"

"You left me, Vest!" she cries while locking another in place towards my chest. "You lied to me! I thought I was going mad! And now...now you expect me to not let this king die?"

I feel a few tears fall from my cheek.

"Everything I do, Vesten."

"Amara." I lift my sword up with both hands. *"Don't do it."*

"I do for the benefit of us!"

She attempts to release another arrow, but with one swift spin, I swing the blade around. The sword's bright orange blade slides directly into the centre of her chest with lightning bolts exploding out towards the bedroom and knocking down some books.

I release my grasp from the sword and look down into her eyes. The bright green irises stare up at me while blood pours from the lower part of her lip onto my hands and into her hair. One of my hands is on her neck and the other on her cheek as she takes some of her last breaths.

"Amarille, please!" I yell, sliding the blade out of her chest and throwing it off to the side so I can hold her on the ground. "Don't do this to me, don't do this to me, Amarille, please. I can't do any of this without you. Have this be another dream, have this be another test, have it be me instead of you!"

Our baby still continues to cry.

26

EPILOGUE

FORTY YEARS LATER...

The sheets I buried my wife in are the same color as her wedding dress.

I spent a few hours shovelling a hole next to where they buried my father. A few hours in which I did nothing but cry and think.

When I close my eyes, I can see her. When I wake up, I pray to The Keeper that she will show up once more and declare this was a final test and there is nothing left to do except go home and be with her.

No man should have to bury someone he loves.

No man should live a life without his wife or son.

To smell the faint perfume in the bed sheet while asleep, to wake up in a haze thinking they may have returned.

When I hold my sword, I can only see her. I can only see the man I have become.

Even now…a couple of years older. I sit down at the bottom of the hill and speak to them as if they will answer me.

One look up at the home at the top of the hill to see my new family, staring as if it were a puzzle missing the last piece.

"I am sorry, my love." I whisper while I trace my hand over the dirt. Everything still feels as fresh as the day she died. "I am trying *so hard* to be a good man."

"And you are, Dad." Vesten the 3rd behind me walks down to sit with me.

Vesten The 3rd is much older now. Maybe even the same age I was when I met Elliot. He has a husband of his own who sits at the top of the house practicing his lightning quirk. All the while, Ariadnen, their son, draws his bow and looses a couple shots into a rotted tree.

"You're thinking of her?" He places a hand on my shoulder.

"Always, Vest," I sigh. A lump in my throat.

A few minutes pass without either of us saying a word. I break the silence, "Have…have I been a good dad?"

I turn to face my son with a few tears falling from my face. He is very quick to wipe them away with his palm.

"I didn't know Mother." He wraps one arm around me. "Dad, there are a lot of bad parents in this world. Kids orphaned, burned by Slimhixe, purists that do not believe the word of the king. A king **you** had a direct part in bringing to power, might I add."

"Little shit." I laugh thinking of my boy Eli trying to run a country. Forever trapped as the young boy from the beach in my mind.

"You were not only the best father to me…but to him." He looks back at our family at the top of the hill. "You taught me how to use a sword but for protection, not vanity. You taught me to love my family, and you taught me that no matter who someone is…they are never lost."

I want to say something but decide against it.

"Let's go back inside, it is gonna be dark soon, Vest."

I attempt to lift myself up before he reaches an arm under mine and helps me up.

"I had it—"

"I know, I know," he says as he leads me up the steps.

I look over at him, his long red beard and few scars. His eyes are more like Amara's than they are mine. He wields *Erron* on his hip, which I inspect for any scratches, but it seems he has kept it in more than mint condition after all these years.

The sky turns an inhuman dark color with what seems like a swift blink of the eyes. Everyone now gathered inside, I wait at the door as my son walks in.

Ariadnen was a teenager, around the same age as Elliot, when we first met. He had a spring to his step and a constant smile.

Henrik, Vesten's husband, brings him in for a kiss. They smile over at me while I give one back, the three of them off to their own conversation.

I turn around and stare out the open door at the sky, which now seems to have turned a feigned red.

Something is not right. Is this a vision? Another test?

The rain that pours down is falling faster than typical water, more viscous, and has a tinge of a color to it I cannot identify.

I reach my right hand out to the rain. It feels wrong. A singing pain like sticking a hand in hot coals...but it feels ever so inviting. Slowly bringing my whole body out into the red rain, I feel the stinging switch from my skin to my lungs and brain.

I take a few more steps down the stairs as the blood finds its way into my nose and eyes. As the pain progressively gets worse and worse, all I do is grunt. Getting down the steps, I look at Amarille's grave.

Only I see her. Untouched by the rain, she smiles. Untouched by my blade, she is perfect.

I hear shouting to me from the top of the hill but it sounds as if they are under water due to the blood finding its way into my ear. I turn back for a brief moment and see the horrified faces of my family at the top of the hill.

Ariadnen tries to run down to me while Henrik and Vesten the 3rd keep him back and beg me to come back inside.

A swift pop in my ears like I have reached an elevated altitude and I smile at them.

"Can you see her?" I yell to them.

"Father, please! Father, come back! Something is not right!" Vesten screams.

"I can see her, Vest. I can see her so clearly you would think she never left."

"Grandfather, please!" Ariadnen squeals. "There is no one there! It's in your head! Come back!"

I lift my head up to the rain and smile wide. I have done everything I can for my family. It's their turn now.

"Tell Elliot I love him!" I whisper, "He may not get the goodbye."

I feel Amarille's hands wrap around my neck and bring my face down to meet hers.

"What took you so long, *Froh'v*?" she whispers.

"I—" I choke on my words, crying. "I have wanted to see you for *so long* my love."

"Why didn't you?"

"I had to make sure our children were okay."

"Are you coming now?" She brushes her hand along my cheek.

Her hand is warm, inviting, and smells a way that I have missed for so long. If this is a dream, another test...why does it feel so nice?

She kisses my lips and I feel all the pain surge into me at once. I fall to my knees and laugh in agony with a wide smile and tears running down my cheeks. Amara follows me down and brings me in for a hug.

"I will never leave you again, Amara," I whisper through gritted teeth.

"Everything we have done *Froh'v*—"

"We have done for us."

"No, Vest." She turns my head to look at our crying family at the top of the stairs. "We have done for **them**."

"I am ready to die," I whisper, falling onto my back, staring up at the red-tinged sky. "I am ready to see you and Erron again."

Amara lifts her body over and onto mine, placing her head against my chest, still unaffected by the red rain. It feels like all the pain is gone as the viscous blood pours over my face, as it slowly covers me and the pain is replaced by a relaxing sense in the muscles. Like slipping into a warm bath.

The red rain from my visions has come to pass....and now I can go see my wife and son.

"Amara...I love y—"

...

Vesten and Elliot Will Return In
Travel Without A Choice
The First Book In The Froh'v Trilogy.

ABOUT THE AUTHOR

Nik Fults was born in Newmarket, Ontario. He often finds himself caught up in his own imagination and endless variety of worlds. You can find Nik usually drinking as much tea as possible, playing video games, or talking with his best friend, a small orange cat named Dexter.

His most popular and debut novel "Sisters Of Blood & Fire." Became an Amazon best-selling novel in the first few days of being made available.

You can follow Nik on Twitter and Instagram: @Authornikfults

Authornikfults.com

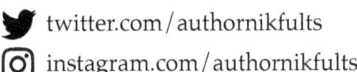

twitter.com/authornikfults
instagram.com/authornikfults

And as always…Keepers Blessings.

www.ingramcontent.com/pod-product-compliance
Lightning Source LLC
LaVergne TN
LVHW012043070526
838202LV00056B/5574